*A Candlelight
Ecstasy Romance*®

"MAKE YOUR CHOICE, MEG.
IT'S HIM OR ME."

Clay's arms crushed her to him. With an angry hunger his lips descended on hers. "Does he make you feel like this? Does he make your heart pound and your body clamor for more?"

Meg pulled away. "It's none of your business. You're just jealous," she accused him.

"Of course I'm jealous. I told you last night that you belong to me now, and I meant it."

"I don't belong to anyone!" she cried angrily.

"That's where you're wrong. You may not admit it, Meg, but you love me as much as I love you. *I'm* the man you want. And I don't intend to share you!"

CANDLELIGHT ECSTASY ROMANCES®

ONE LOVE FOREVER

Christine King

A CANDLELIGHT ECSTASY ROMANCE®

Published by
Dell Publishing Co., Inc.
1 Dag Hammarskjold Plaza
New York, New York 10017

ISBN: 0-440-16608-X

Printed in the United States of America

July 1986

10 9 8 7 6 5 4 3 2 1

WFH

To Barbara Barger,
who leaped into the breach
at the last moment
and saved the day.

To Our Readers:

We have been delighted with your enthusiastic response to Candlelight Ecstasy Romances®, and we thank you for the interest you have shown in this exciting series.

In the upcoming months we will continue to present the distinctive sensuous love stories you have come to expect only from Ecstasy. We look forward to bringing you many more books from your favorite authors and also the very finest work from new authors of contemporary romantic fiction.

As always, we are striving to present the unique, absorbing love stories that you enjoy most—books that are more than ordinary romance. Your suggestions and comments are always welcome. Please write to us at the address below.

Sincerely,

The Editors
Candlelight Romances
1 Dag Hammarskjold Plaza
New York, New York 10017

CHAPTER ONE

This wasn't the way it was supposed to be, Meg thought nervously as she started down the aisle of the small church she had attended as a child. Something was missing. Beneath the beautiful white wedding gown she was wearing, her heart should have been pounding with joy and her spirits should have been soaring. This was her wedding day. She was about to become Mrs. Henry Johnson.

Why, then, were her feet so heavy that she could barely put one in front of the other? Why did she feel an impulse to turn and run?

After what seemed like an interminable walk, Meg reached the end of the aisle. Henry smiled, but he didn't seem real to her. His face wasn't quite clear. She felt as though she were looking at it from a distance. In a daze, she listened to the minister, and as she listened, her panic grew.

What was she doing here? she asked herself wildly. This was all a mistake—a terrible mistake.

". . . If there is any man here who can show just cause why these two should not be joined together, let him speak now or—"

"Meg!"—a man's voice called commandingly from the pews behind her—"Don't do it!"

The minister broke off in shocked surprise, and a startled hush fell over the congregation.

"You'll regret this for the rest of your life," the man's voice went on urgently. "Don't do it!"

All at once, the congregation began to buzz with whispered conjecture. Meg stared straight ahead, her heart pounding. She was afraid to turn and look.

"Who is that?" Henry hissed.

"I don't know," she replied faintly. She did know, though. She hadn't heard that voice in seven years, but it didn't matter. She'd recognize it after a hundred years, a thousand years.

Slowly, she turned to face the man who was making a shambles of her wedding. There, standing in the middle of the aisle, looking supremely unconcerned about the whispers and startled glances, was Clay Beaumont. As a child, she had idolized him. By the time she was eighteen, her hero worship had turned to love—unrequited love. Now he stood in front of her looking ridiculously handsome and larger than ever in the small church. As her confused blue eyes met his blazing black ones, she felt her heart turn over. They stared at each other in silence until the church and everyone in it seemed to disappear. As far as Meg was concerned, there was no one in the universe but the two of them. Happiness, like a shooting fountain, began to spurt through her. Her eyes were still fixed on his when Clay strode masterfully down the aisle and swept her into his arms.

"You're coming with me," he said in a harsh voice that brooked no argument.

Completely unmindful of the pandemonium that had broken out, he carried her back down the aisle and out of the church. He paused for a moment on the steps and gently lifted her veil. Meg looked up at him with her heart in her eyes. He smiled the crooked smile she remembered so well and bent his head to kiss her. Just as his lips were about to touch hers, she woke up.

"Damn," she said softly. "I didn't want to wake up."

She sat up and stared into the darkness. Her entire body trembled.

Clay Beaumont. What had made her dream of him after all this time? She hadn't thought about him in at least two years, she told herself untruthfully.

She knew why she had dreamed of the wedding. That was easy enough to explain. A few hours earlier, after a year and a half of courtship, Henry Johnson had proposed. On the point of saying yes, something had stopped Meg, and she had asked for a few days to think it over instead.

She liked Henry. She supposed she even loved him, after a fashion. Theirs was a comfortable relationship. It was true that there was little romance or passion between them, but then, Meg wasn't interested in passion. At eighteen, she had discovered how glorious, and how ultimately heartrending, love and passion could be. She never wanted to experience that kind of pain again. Never! She didn't hear bells when Henry kissed her, and her heart didn't flutter when he walked into the room, but she didn't let those things bother her. She and Henry got along well together. They had similar tastes and they rarely argued. If that wasn't mature adult love, what was?

Why, then, had Clay suddenly popped out of her subconscious? He hadn't been a part of her life for seven years. Psychiatrists would undoubtedly say that a dream like that was full of significance, she told herself crossly as she punched her pillow and settled herself back down into the bed. If it was, she didn't want to know about it.

Morning finally dawned. Meg hadn't slept a wink after that strange dream. Instead, she had lain there tossing and turning—and trying not to think about Clay and

11

how real he had seemed as he bent to kiss her. When she finally got out of bed, she was tired and irritable.

She ate breakfast hurriedly, got dressed, and just before she left for the beginning of one of her hectic days, she made a call to the ranch outside Houston where her Aunt Helen lived. Ever since the death of her uncle last month, Meg had called her aunt each morning. Helen was like a mother to Meg. She and her husband, John, had taken Meg in when her parents died, and all the happiness and security Meg had felt as a child were due entirely to them. She was sure no parents could have been more loving. Now she wanted to help her aunt in any way she could.

"How are you this morning?" Meg asked when her aunt picked up the phone.

"I'm fine," Helen told her. She said that every morning.

Meg didn't believe her. Her aunt and uncle had been devoted to one another, and she knew Helen was having a very difficult time adjusting to being alone. Now Meg thought her aunt's cheerfulness sounded a little forced.

"Is anything wrong?" she asked anxiously.

"No, of course not," her aunt replied. "What could be wrong?"

"I don't know," Meg told her. "I thought you sounded worried about something."

"It must be the connection," Helen said. "How was your date with Henry?"

"It was very nice," Meg said listlessly. "We went to dinner and a movie."

"Did he get around to popping the question?" Helen had been asking that particular question for the past six months, until it had become something of a joke.

Meg hesitated for a moment. "As a matter of fact, he did," she said finally.

"That's wonderful!" Helen cried. "I just knew he'd get

12

up the nerve to ask you sooner or later. When are you going to be married?"

"We aren't," Meg said flatly. How could she marry one man when she dreamed of another?

"You aren't?" her aunt repeated incredulously. "But I thought you were in love with him."

"I care for him, of course," Meg said, "but I don't think I'm in love with him."

"Are you sure you know what you're doing?" Helen asked anxiously. "Perhaps you've simply been working too hard. I'm sure once you've had time to think about it, you'll realize what a suitable marriage it would be. He's an up-and-coming lawyer, and he'll always be able to provide for you."

"I don't need anyone to provide for me," Meg said. "I'm perfectly capable of providing for myself."

"Of course you are," Helen said soothingly. "But what about children? I know you want a family."

Meg did want a family. With every day that passed, she wanted one a little more.

"You're right," she said. "I do want a family, and Henry would be a good husband and a good father. But I just don't feel about him the way you felt about Uncle John."

There was a silence at the other end of the phone; then her aunt spoke. "In that case," she said quietly, "there's nothing more to be said. As long as you're sure."

"I am sure," Meg assured her. "I should be. I was up most of last night thinking about it."

"Then you haven't told him your decision yet?"

"No." Meg sighed. "I asked for a couple of days to think it over."

"If you needed a few days to think it over," her aunt said dryly, "you can hardly be madly in love."

"That's the conclusion I finally came to," Meg said. "But I do care for him, and I don't want to hurt him."

"I know you don't," Helen said. "But it's better this

13

way. If you married him feeling as you do, you'd be cheating him and yourself out of something very wonderful."

"I suppose you're right," Meg said wearily.

"Of course I'm right," Helen told her. "Now, the thing for you to do is to get out and meet new men."

Meg groaned. "I don't want to meet new men. I don't have time for that."

"You've got to make time. How else are you going to meet Mr. Right?"

"I'm not even sure he exists," Meg retorted.

"I found him and so will you," her aunt replied with perfect confidence. "But you've got to make an effort. You're not getting any younger, you know."

"I'm only twenty-five," Meg protested, "and my career—"

"I know your career is important," Helen interrupted, "but I can't help worrying about you. Your career is wearing you out. You work twelve hours a day, and for what? Not for money, that's for sure. You're not getting rich that I can see."

Meg laughed. "No, I'm certainly not. But I love what I do. I get a lot of satisfaction out of it."

"I'm sure you do. But is it enough to make up for not having a home and a family?"

"I have a home," Meg said mildly. "Two, if you count the ranch."

"You know what I mean," Helen replied firmly.

Meg did know. There were days when she wondered if all the work, all the long hours she put in were really worth anything. She wasn't going to tell her aunt that, however. Her aunt worried enough about her as it was.

"My problem is that I want it all," she told her aunt lightly. "I want my career and a family. Speaking of my career, I've got to run. I've got a taping this morning." *Cooking with Meg*, the TV show that had turned Meg

14

into something of a local celebrity, aired three mornings a week on a local station.

"You'll call me tomorrow, won't you?" Helen suddenly sounded lonely.

"Of course," Meg promised.

As she hung up the phone, her eyes filled with unexpected tears. The loneliness in Helen's voice had upset her. Not only that, she sensed that Helen was worrying about something. She had sounded cheerful enough, but there had been something in her voice that sounded forced.

Meg sighed. She knew Helen wouldn't tell her what it was until she was ready. If only Helen would sell the ranch and move to Houston, she thought. But every time Meg brought up the subject, her aunt refused to even consider it. She had lived on the ranch for forty-five years, she said, and all her memories were there. She'd die if she had to leave it.

Meg glanced at her watch, which seemed to rule her life lately, then jumped to her feet with a gasp. Thursday was her busiest day, and she couldn't afford to start out behind schedule. After her session at the TV station, she had to rush over to La Bonne Femme, the fashionable French restaurant where she was the head chef. Although the owner of the restaurant was delighted with the publicity Meg's show brought his restaurant and didn't mind the time she took off for her tapings, Meg hated the extra work that her absence created for the other employees of the restaurant.

She hurried over to the TV station and found that the day, which had started off so poorly, was getting worse. Everything that could go wrong did. For some reason she kept dropping things, and she couldn't keep her mind on the food she was preparing.

It wasn't until she was alone in her dressing room, removing the makeup she wore for the camera, that she

15

allowed herself to think of Clay. She couldn't keep her thoughts at bay any longer.

He had grown up on Broken Rock Ranch, the ranch that adjoined her aunt and uncle's land. Meg had known him for most of her life, certainly for as long as she could remember. Clay and her uncle had been very close, and her uncle had often said that Clay was the kind of son any man would be proud to have. Clay was nine years older than Meg, and he seemed to live in a different world. He had always been kind to her, though, and he had even teased her in a brotherly way—until the summer before her nineteenth birthday. Then everything had changed.

Meg absently smoothed some cold cream onto her face and let her mind drift back to that summer. She had been just home from her first year of college. Clay had stopped by to pick up something from her uncle and had wandered out to the patio where Meg was sunbathing. She still remembered the way Clay's eyes had widened as he saw her lying in the sun in her bikini.

"You've grown up," he drawled as his eyes took in all her curves.

"I was grown up before," she said a little irritably. "You just didn't notice." Something in the way he was looking at her made her uncomfortable.

"Well, I'm noticing now. I must have been out of my mind not to notice before. How old are you, honey?"

He had always called her honey, but now it sounded different.

"I'm eighteen," she told him.

"And I'm twenty-seven," he said regretfully.

"Are you trying to tell me I'm too young for you?" Meg asked. The look on his face was giving her confidence that she had never felt before.

He shook his head and gave her a slow grin. "No. I'm telling you I'm too old for you."

"Are you sure?" she asked. "I might surprise you."

16

She couldn't believe she was talking like this—to Clay Beaumont, of all people.

"I'm more likely to surprise you," he told her. "I'm not one of your eighteen-year-old boyfriends. There's a world of experience between them and me, and some of it might shock you."

Meg had looked into his eyes, expecting to see that he was laughing at her. Instead, he seemed serious, almost somber. She stared back at him, not knowing how to answer.

"Here are those papers you wanted, Clay," her uncle had broken in. He came out onto the patio. "I see you've found Margaret."

"I certainly have," Clay said. "Would you mind if I took her to a movie tonight?"

Meg's Uncle John had hesitated, and it was clear to Meg that he was thinking of Clay's age and his growing reputation as a ladies' man.

"No, I guess not," he said finally. "After all, you're a friend of the family. Just remember that she's only eighteen."

Meg blushed, partly out of embarrassment and partly in anger. They were both treating her like a child, and she didn't like it.

"Why don't you ask me if I'd like to go to a movie with you?" she said to Clay.

He looked down at her, and his eyes were suddenly laughing. "All right, I will. Will you go out with me tonight?"

It would serve him right if I said no, she thought, although she knew she'd never forgive herself if she turned down a chance to go out with Clay Beaumont.

"I'd like that," she said instead.

"Good. I'll pick you up at seven thirty. And don't worry," he said, turning to John, "I'll have her back early."

For years she'd had a crush on Clay; for years she had

dreamed about him. Now her dreams were going to come true!

They had dated for the rest of the summer. As her aunt and uncle watched with concern, her crush deepened into love. "You're too young to be serious about anyone," they cautioned her over and over again. "And Clay is too old for you." Her aunt warned her repeatedly about Clay's reputation with women, but Meg paid no attention. She listened politely of course, but nothing they said made any difference. She loved Clay and, although he never said it, she was beginning to think he loved her.

The two of them took long walks, they rode horseback all over his ranch and hers, and they picnicked by the small, sometimes dry stream that separated Broken Rock from her uncle's land. All during that time, Clay treated her with the utmost respect. Their kisses were light and chaste, and although she occasionally caught him looking longingly at her, he never attempted anything her aunt and uncle would not have approved of—that is, not until the week before she was to return to college.

That night, when he picked her up, he was unusually quiet. Instead of the movie they had planned on seeing, Clay asked if she would mind going down by the creek where they could talk.

He was going to propose, Meg thought ecstatically. She was sure of it. Her heart began pounding against her rib cage with such force that she could hardly answer.

But when he had spread out a blanket for them to sit on, he fell silent. Meg sat quietly beside him until she couldn't stand it any longer. She slipped her hand into his, and at her touch he turned and gave her his crooked smile.

She smiled back tremulously, thinking that now he would say the words she longed to hear.

Instead, he began talking about her return to college.

"When you get back to college," he had said, "I want

you to forget all about me. I want you to go out with boys your own age and have a good time."

For Meg, the night had suddenly turned cold.

"I was wrong to take up so much of your time this summer," Clay went on. "I should have seen to it that you went out with boys closer to your own age."

She stared at him. "Haven't you enjoyed going out with me?" she asked in a faltering voice. She was too shocked by his words to hide her feelings.

At the sound in her voice, he turned and looked down at her. In the moonlight, he could see the hurt in her eyes. He put his arm around her and hugged her tightly for a brief moment.

"I've enjoyed every minute we've spent together. More than—" He broke off and began again. "But it hasn't been fair to you. You've got to go back to college and forget me."

"I could never forget you," she said in a low tone. She was beginning to ache all over.

Clay leaned over and kissed her swiftly. It was unlike the other kisses he had given her. As their lips met, Meg could feel his desire for her, and also his frustration.

"That's sweet of you to say, but you're young. You'll forget me very quickly."

"You're wrong," she said quietly. She felt as though her heart would break.

His arm tightened around her shoulders. "I wish I were. But you're only eighteen."

"I may be only eighteen," she told him in a voice that was beginning to tremble, "but I know what I feel. And I—"

He covered her mouth with his hand. "Don't say anything you'll regret later," he warned her.

Meg took his hand in her own and kissed it. "If you won't let me tell you how I feel, maybe you'll let me show you." She turned so that she faced him, then put her arms around his neck.

19

"Don't tempt me, Meg," he said with a little groan. "I'm only human. All summer long I've had to force myself to keep my hands off you."

"I don't want you to keep your hands off me." Later she would be embarrassed by what she was saying, but now she only wanted to be in his arms. "I want you to kiss me, to love me," she breathed.

His mouth drew closer to hers. "You don't know the first thing about love," he muttered hoarsely.

"Then teach me," she whispered. "Show me how to please you."

"I'd like to, honey," he said a little unsteadily, "I'd like to very much. But—" He suddenly swore softly under his breath, then crushed her to him.

Meg gasped as his lips closed over hers. This was a kiss unlike anything she had ever experienced, and it swept reality away with its force. Before she quite knew what was happening, she and Clay were lying on the blanket. Meg turned in his arms and pressed herself against the length of his body. She ran her trembling fingers through his hair. Clay responded with a hungry kiss that parted her lips and gave him possession of her mouth.

"I don't want to go back to college," she whispered. "I don't want to leave you."

"You have to," he muttered hoarsely.

"Why?" she managed to ask. Her voice had grown as unsteady as her breathing.

He didn't answer. He wasn't interested in conversation. Instead, his lips began exploring the hollows of her neck. Impatiently, he pulled her blouse free and slipped his large warm hands underneath it. As he touched her bare skin, Meg tensed. Then their lips met in a long, exquisite kiss, and she felt herself melt against him. For a moment she thought she would faint from the intensity of her feelings. She had never known such rapture could exist. She was being consumed by desires that should

20

have frightened her but, because she was with Clay, didn't.

"Little Meg," he muttered as his mouth gently brushed her eyes, her nose, and the sensitive spot behind her ears. "Sweet little Meg. I've wanted to do this since the day I saw you in that skimpy bikini."

"I've wanted it, too," Meg murmured. She looked into his dark eyes and saw intense, demanding hunger. Her breath caught, and she wound her arms around his neck and pulled him closer. "Kiss me again," she whispered in his ear.

Again their lips locked in a seemingly endless kiss. Meg felt as though she were drowning in new sensations. She reveled in the feel of his hands on her skin and in his warmth and closeness. Without realizing what she was doing, her yearning body twisted itself against him. In response, she felt a tremor go through him.

"I can't stop now," he muttered.

She wasn't sure whether he was talking to her or to himself.

"I don't want you to," she breathed.

From that moment, she was lost in the passion Clay was so expertly creating. Nothing else seemed to matter.

"I love you," she whispered finally. Her voice seemed to speak of its own volition. She wouldn't have thought she had the strength to speak.

Clay pulled away a little and gazed at her. His dark eyes probed hers, and for a moment she thought he was going to say he loved her. She stared back at him, almost willing him to say the words she so desperately wanted to hear. Instead, he pulled his hands from beneath her blouse and smoothed it down.

"You're too young to love anyone," he said lightly, "least of all someone nine years older than you."

Meg felt as though she had been slapped. She pulled away and forced back the tears that were threatening to fill her eyes.

21

"If you think I'm such a child," she said as icily as she could while she fought for control of her breathing, "what was that all about?"

He shrugged and got to his feet. "I brought you down here to tell you good-bye. I didn't mean for this to happen. But I'm a man. I'm very much a man, as you almost found out."

Meg hoped she wasn't blushing. She scrambled to her feet and they stared at each other. The rumpled blanket lay between them.

"What else did you think would happen when you threw yourself at me?" he asked.

"I didn't throw myself at you!" she cried.

He gave her a considering look. "Well, you didn't exactly run away. And once I had you in my arms, I didn't want to let you go. You're a beautiful girl. In a few years, you'll be a beautiful and desirable woman. I hope I'll be around to see it. Perhaps then we can finish what we started."

With each word he spoke, Meg felt as though a knife were being twisted into her heart. He didn't love her. She didn't mean anything to him. He had just been amusing himself with her for the summer.

She didn't remember anything about the trip home. As they pulled up in front of the house, Clay put his hand on her arm and gave her a somber look.

"It's better this way," he told her. "In the morning you'll be glad nothing happened."

Meg wrenched her arm away and got out of the car without saying a word. She didn't trust herself to speak. She was afraid anything she might say would betray her pain and humiliation.

A week later, she was back at college. Getting settled wasn't made any easier by the letters she received from her aunt and uncle. In each letter, Clay was paired with a different woman, and her aunt frequently commented on Clay's growing reputation as a ladies' man.

22

Finally, Meg received a letter from Clay himself. It was a short, friendly letter, the kind of letter a man would write to the kid sister of a friend. Hurt and angry, she wrote back, telling him she had recently become pinned to a fraternity man she had met. It wasn't true, of course, and although Meg knew she wasn't being very mature, she wanted to hit back.

Clay didn't write again, and she was just as glad. Even the sight of his handwriting hurt her. When Christmas came, she couldn't go home but went to stay with a friend instead so that she wouldn't be anywhere near him. She didn't want anything to aggravate the wound that refused to heal.

In her small dressing room now, Meg sat with her head in her hands. For six years after that, she had been haunted by Clay. Then, during the last year or so, she thought she had finally managed to push him from her thoughts. Last night's dream showed her how wrong she had been. Clay haunted her still, as did memories of the passion they had shared, passion so intense that, seven years later, it still had the power to make her tremble.

She looked over at the clock. She was due at the restaurant in ten minutes, and it was a good half-hour away. Those few minutes she had spent daydreaming had put her behind schedule. She grabbed her pocketbook, ran out the door, and drove straight into a traffic jam. By the time she reached La Bonne Femme, she was hot, irritable, and an hour late.

This is no way to live, she thought as she began racing the clock in preparation for the restaurant's first customers.

It seemed as though the night would never end. The air conditioning was on the blink, and there was an unusually large crowd for a Thursday night.

"I don't know why anyone would be a chef," she said to the dishwasher after she had pushed a strand of her damp hair from her face. "We're here slaving away while the rest of the world is relaxing."

He merely grinned at her. He, like everyone else in the restaurant, knew that she loved her work.

"Meg," said Jake Rhinehart, the owner of the restaurant, "one of the customers would like to see you for a moment. I think he wants to present his compliments in person."

"Can't you tell him I'm busy?" she asked wearily. "Look at me. I'm a mess." Her gently curling hair had wilted in the heat and humidity of the kitchen, and she was wearing no makeup at all.

"All you need is a clean apron and you'll look fine," Jake told her firmly. "He's an important customer. He eats here at least once a week, and he's a big spender. He's never asked to speak to you before. I don't want to offend him."

Meg sighed and put on a clean apron.

"He says he's a fan of yours," Jake threw over his shoulder as he led her into the restaurant's reception area.

Meg stopped dead in her tracks. She felt the world tilt violently, then steady itself. The "fan" was none other than Clay Beaumont. He was with a glamorous redhead who was wearing an expensive green sheath dress.

Oh no, Meg thought in horror. It can't be Clay. Not today, of all days. She wanted to turn and run.

She had often imagined what it would be like to meet him. In her imaginings, she had always been beautifully dressed and she had carried herself with a sophisticated air that showed him how little he meant to her after all this time. But now, instead of being poised and composed, she was staring at him in shocked surprise.

Abruptly, she pulled herself together. He didn't mean anything to her anymore, and she didn't have to prove that to anyone, least of all to him.

"Hello, Clay," she said evenly.

24

"Hello, Meg," he returned easily. "It's been a long time."

Not long enough, she wanted to say.

"I didn't know you two knew each other," Jake exclaimed.

"Oh, we're old friends," Clay told him. His eyes were still on Meg's face.

Jake hesitated, then tactfully drew the redhead away so that the two of them could talk alone.

"Who is she?" Meg asked, simply for something to say. She already knew the answer. Clay was practically a legend in Houston. He was rich, powerful, attractive, and almost as well-known for his girl friends as he was for his spectacular business deals.

Clay's eyebrows rose. "Elaine's not my wife, if that's what you're asking."

That wasn't what she was asking. If Clay had gotten married anytime in the past seven years, all of Houston—including Meg—would have known it.

"Hasn't your aunt kept you up on the local gossip?" he asked with a lazy grin.

"We have better things to talk about than you," she told him. Actually, she had always changed the subject whenever his name was mentioned. The less she heard about him, the better.

"Do you?" he asked mildly. A tiny, infuriating grin appeared on his face. "You have flour on your cheek." He raised his hand and brushed it off with his thumb. His fingers seemed to linger on her face.

Meg stepped back. She felt as though she had been shocked.

Clay's grin disappeared, and he became serious. "I was sorry to hear about your uncle," he told her. "I would have gone to the funeral, but I was out of the country. I only got back a few days ago."

Meg nodded. "Aunt Helen wondered why you weren't

25

there. She and Uncle John were always very fond of you."

He smiled mirthlessly, and for one brief moment Meg thought she saw bitterness in that smile. She told herself she must be mistaken. There had never been anything in his relationship with her aunt and uncle to make him bitter.

"I saw Helen as soon as I returned. She misses you."

"I know she does," Meg said steadily. "I've asked her to consider selling the ranch and moving to Houston, but she won't even think about it."

"Is there any chance of you moving back there?"

She shook her head. "This is my home now."

"I suppose you're too much the television star to go back to living on a ranch," he said. Meg looked into his eyes. The mockery she saw there annoyed her.

"That's not true at all," she snapped.

"I'm glad to hear it." He started to say more, but the redhead had rejoined them and taken possession of his arm.

"Are you ready to go, handsome?" she purred. She didn't bother to acknowledge Meg's presence.

Clay smiled down at her, and Meg suddenly had the feeling she had been shut out.

"I'm ready," he murmured.

When he turned back to Meg, his voice was suddenly polite. "I just wanted to tell you how much I enjoy your cooking." It was very obvious that he had the redhead on his mind now, not Meg. Meg got the message loud and clear.

"Thank you," she said stiffly. She had been dismissed, and she didn't like it. She stared at the two of them, wondering if she could possibly be jealous after all these years. It wasn't a pleasant thought.

Clay gave her an amused smile. He seemed to know

26

what she was thinking. He slipped his arm around the redhead's waist.

"I'll call you one of these days. We can talk over old times," he said as they turned to go. "Good night, Meg."

Meg stared after him in silence.

CHAPTER TWO

The ringing of the phone woke her. Meg grabbed it and held it to her ear.

"Good morning, Meg," the voice at the other end said.

Clay! She sat up in bed and rested her head against her hand. "What time is it?" she asked.

"It's seven thirty."

"Seven thirty," she repeated incredulously. "Why are you calling me so early on a Sunday morning? For that matter, why are you calling me at all?" She hadn't meant to say that; the words just seemed to slip out on their own.

"Is that any way to talk to me after seven long years?" he asked with a soft chuckle.

"Look, Clay, I didn't get in until late last night and—"

"Did you have a hot date?" he inquired casually.

"No," she snapped. "Saturday night is our big night at the restaurant. I'm a working girl, remember? And Sunday is the only time I have to catch up on my sleep. Why did you call?"

There was a pause, then his voice turned serious. "I have to talk to you."

"I can't imagine anything we might have to talk about."

"Can't you?" he asked mildly. "I can. But, at this moment, I've got some business to discuss with you."

"All right," she said. "Start talking."

"It's not something we can discuss on the phone. I'm on my way back to the ranch and—"

"At this hour?" she asked in spite of herself. "What happened? Did your redhead throw you out?"

"Do I detect a note of jealousy?" he asked.

"You most certainly do not."

"Are you sure about that? Your eyes were spitting fire when you saw her last Thursday."

"That's ridiculous."

"I'm not so sure," he said teasingly. "I got the idea that my way with women bothers you."

"Then you got the wrong idea," she said icily. She took a deep breath. "Look, Clay, we haven't seen each other in seven years. I'm not interested in your women. As a matter of fact, there's a rather special man in my life at the moment and—"

"Do you mean the man you just refused to marry?" he asked blandly.

Meg almost dropped the receiver. "How did you know about that?"

"Helen told me," he replied smoothly. "She and I had a nice long talk about you."

Blast my aunt, Meg thought irritably. She felt like a prize idiot.

"Aren't you wondering how I got your phone number?"

"I'm in the phone book," she said coolly. "We're getting away from the point of this call, aren't we? What do you want to talk about?"

"Not over the phone," he reminded her. "I'm only two blocks away from your apartment. I thought I could stop by on my way out of town."

29

"Don't be ridiculous." Her voice rose slightly. "I'm in bed."

"I know. Why do you think I called so early?" he asked wickedly.

In the pause that followed, Meg knew they were both thinking of that night seven years ago. She rubbed her forehead with her free hand, hoping to banish those memories.

"You can't stop by now," she said stiffly. "I can't possibly be dressed by the time you get here."

"I'll help you," he offered. "You probably don't know it, but I'm very good around the house."

Meg felt herself growing angry. "I don't see any point to this conversation," she told him. "I'm tired, and I want to go back to sleep."

"Alone?"

"Yes, alone," she snapped.

"I was afraid you'd say that." His voice sounded regretful. "In that case, I'll stop by this evening. We can go out to dinner."

"I can't have dinner with you," Meg said quickly.

She didn't want to be around him any more than she had to be. In fact, she didn't want to be around him at all.

"Sunday is a busy day for me. If you really have something important to talk about, you can stop by for a few minutes this evening. Otherwise—"

"Otherwise, you don't want to see me again," he said, his voice suddenly cold. "Is that it?"

Meg closed her eyes. "If you want the truth, yes," she said, trying to ignore the feelings in her that suggested otherwise.

"You still haven't forgiven me for what happened seven years ago," he said wistfully.

"There's nothing to forgive," she told him wearily. "I forgot all about it as soon as I got back to college."

"I've never forgotten about it," he said quietly.

Meg made her voice light. "Haven't you? That surprises me. With all the women at your beck and call, you don't need to go around seducing eighteen-year-old girls."

"I didn't seduce you, Meg. I didn't need to. You were more than willing."

That was the last thing she wanted to think of now. She was haunted enough by memories of Clay as it was. "I really don't remember much of that night," she said quickly. "It was so long ago. What time do you want to stop by?"

"How does eight o'clock sound?"

"That's fine. But I want to warn you, I go to bed early."

"Is that an invitation?"

"No, it isn't," she snapped.

He sighed. "Another time, then."

"Clay!"

He chuckled. "See you tonight, honey."

She was left holding a dead receiver. She slammed it down, then spent the next thirty minutes trying to go back to sleep. It was no use. When she closed her eyes, she saw Clay, and that was more than enough to bring her wide awake.

In spite of all the laundry and cleaning she had to do, the day seemed to drag by. Meg was tormented by thoughts of Clay. The last few days, beginning with the dream of her marriage to Henry, had taught her just how large a place Clay still had in her heart. Seeing him had brought all the memories she had tried to forget flooding back to her. Even worse, seeing him with that redhead had sparked feelings that shocked and dismayed her. She might not be eighteen anymore, but she was certainly acting like it.

Eight o'clock finally arrived, then eight fifteen. At eight thirty, Meg decided he wasn't coming. She was absurdly disappointed—and furious with herself for feeling

31

that way. Then the doorbell rang and her heart leaped into her throat. She took a deep breath and forced herself to count to ten before she opened it.

"Hello, Meg," Clay said when she finally pulled it open. His eyes ran over her slender body, taking in the gentle curves of her figure.

"Come on in," she said curtly. He was almost looking at her hungrily, she thought, and she didn't like it.

He followed her across the room, and when Meg turned to sit down, she found he was still watching her.

"What are you staring at?" she asked hesitantly, feeling uncomfortable.

"You," he replied. "I see my prediction came true." He sounded almost proud. "You have turned into a beautiful, desirable woman."

His words took Meg straight back to that hot, breathless night seven years ago.

"You said you had some business to discuss," she said quickly. "What is it?"

He laughed and sat down as if he owned the place. "Not so fast. First I want you to tell me how you are and what you've been doing these last few years. We have a lot of catching up to do."

"I'm fine." She sat down in a chair across from him. "You know what I've been doing. You've been eating my cooking at least once a week for the past two years."

"How did you know that?" he asked absently. His eyes were wandering over her face, and Meg knew her cheeks were flushed under his gaze.

"Jake Rhinehart mentioned that you were a regular customer," she admitted. She didn't want Clay to think she had been discussing him. He was conceited enough as it was.

However, that was exactly what he did think. "So you were curious about me. It sounds like you might be still a little interested, Meg," he drawled.

"No," Meg told him firmly. "I'm not."

"You were once," he reminded her.

"When I was eighteen, I had a crush on you," she told him evenly. "I'm not eighteen anymore."

His eyes moved slowly over her body. "No, you've definitely grown up since then," he said thoughtfully.

"Stop staring at me."

His eyes returned to her face. "Sorry, honey," he drawled. "I didn't mean to make you uncomfortable. The fact is that I like looking at you. It's been a long time."

Whose fault is that? she wanted to ask.

"Since you don't want to tell me what's been going on in your life," he was saying, "I'll tell you what's been going on in mine. I suppose you heard that my father died about six months after you went back to college that year."

"Yes, I did," Meg said in a gentler tone. "I was sorry to hear it. I didn't know him well, of course, but—"

Clay shrugged. "I don't think anyone knew him well, least of all his son."

Meg looked up. She thought she'd caught a hint of vulnerability in his voice. She studied his face carefully. It was leaner—and harder—than it had been seven years ago. There were lines around his eyes and mouth that hadn't existed before. It was a face that gave nothing away. He was definitely not the kind of man to show his emotions; he was too proud to let anyone know if he'd been hurt.

"Still, it must have been quite a shock to you," she probed gently. "He was only fifty-three."

"It was a shock," Clay admitted. Then he shrugged again, as if trying to deny any pain. "But I didn't really see much of him. Your Uncle John was closer to me than my father ever was. John taught me how to ride, how to shoot, how to be a man." Clay's eyes narrowed slightly and his voice was hushed. "Those were things my father never had time to do. Business always came first."

Meg felt her heart tug sympathetically. Clay would

33

probably die rather than admit that his father's indifference had hurt him. His father's neglect had probably gone a long way toward making Clay the proud, self-contained man he was.

"If I ever have a son—" Clay began. He broke off abruptly. "Well, things would be different."

"Don't let it hurt you," Meg said. Impulsively, she leaned forward and put her hand on his arm. "I know your father loved you. He just didn't know how to show it. Some men are like that."

He gave her a grateful glance and took her hand in his own.

"Meg Howard's specialty," he teased gently. "Kindness to dumb animals. I remember how you adopted and mothered every creature that came your way. You haven't changed much."

Their eyes met for a long second, then Meg spoke breathlessly. "You're hardly what I'd call a dumb animal." As she pulled her hand away, she cautioned herself not to get involved with Clay.

"You're right, though. My father couldn't show his feelings. Your uncle was the one who made me see that. I owed him a lot." He looked away suddenly. "And I paid it all back."

"I'm sure you did," she said gently. "He cared for you very much. You were like a son to him."

"That's not what I meant," Clay said shortly.

"Then what did you mean?" Meg was intrigued.

Clay looked at her and shrugged. "It doesn't matter now. Let's just say he asked me for a favor—a favor I've paid for ever since."

Meg had no idea what he was talking about. She gazed at him thoughtfully. This was a new Clay; this was a Clay Beaumont she hadn't known existed. The feeling of sympathy she felt grew stronger, although she tried to resist it. She didn't want to feel sorry for Clay. She didn't want to be that involved. Besides, he was not a man who wanted pity.

"Who's staring now?" he asked, his voice growing so soft it was almost caressing. "Do you like what you see, honey?"

Meg flushed. She ignored his question and the not-too-subtle meaning behind it.

"I didn't mean to stare," she said stiffly. "I was thinking about something."

She wanted him to leave. Even after seven years, he was too adept at stirring up her emotions.

"It's getting late, Clay. I really don't have time to sit here and make polite chitchat."

"I'm not used to women calling the story of my life polite chitchat," he said with a scowl so ferocious and so obviously assumed that Meg had to smile.

"I'm sure you're not," she agreed dryly. "I'm sure the women you know hang on your every word. But I have a million things to do. Why don't you just get to the point of this visit?"

"All right, I will." He hesitated a moment, then asked, "Did you know that your aunt is about to lose her ranch?"

Meg felt the blood drain from her face. "What are you talking about?" she asked sharply.

"Then I take it you didn't know."

She shook her head and leaned forward in her chair. "No, of course not. I don't understand. I thought Uncle John left enough money to take care of her."

"Apparently your uncle had been going through some hard times. He had borrowed quite a bit of money that he couldn't pay back."

"Why didn't he come to me?" Meg asked. "I don't have much, but I would have been happy, more than happy, to give him everything I have. If it weren't for them—"

Clay nodded understandingly. "I know how you feel.

But your uncle was a proud man. He wouldn't have felt right taking money from you, any more than he would have felt right about taking money from me."

Meg bowed her head. "I suppose so. But I would have liked to help."

"You may get your chance," Clay told her. "If you really mean it."

"I do mean it," she told him almost angrily. "You know I do."

He gave her a long hard look. "The bank is threatening to foreclose on your aunt unless she pays back what is owing."

"She can have everything I've got in savings," Meg said immediately. "How much does she need?"

She gasped as he named the figure. Her pale face turned even whiter. He might as well have said a million dollars.

"How in the world did he get into debt for that much money?" she asked dazedly.

"Stock is expensive. He bought a couple of high-priced bulls, and he had a few bad years. If he had lived, I'm sure he would have pulled the ranch out of the red. But your aunt can't do it by herself."

"What about the men who work there?" Meg asked. "Can't they help?"

"She had to let them go."

Meg stared at him in shock. Helen hadn't said a word to her about any of this. "She'll just have to hire someone else," she said finally.

"She could do that, of course, if she could find someone who would work for free. She simply doesn't have any money."

Meg shook her head, trying to clear away the shock of Clay's words. "I thought she sounded worried the last couple of times I talked to her, but she kept saying it was my imagination." She looked up at him. "How do you know all this, anyway? Did Aunt Helen tell you?"

"No. She's as proud as your uncle. She approached the bank in which I hold a large piece of stock, and one of the officers of the bank knows she's a neighbor of mine, so he told me about her loan request."

"Is the bank going to grant it?" Meg asked hopefully.

"No," Clay said flatly.

"Why not?" She got to her feet and began pacing. "How can they refuse her?"

"Very easily," he said dryly. "Banks are in business to make money, and your aunt is a bad risk. She's an older woman living on a ranch she can't possibly manage alone, and she doesn't have any collateral."

"She has the ranch. That's collateral."

He shook his head. "If it were sold tomorrow, it wouldn't pay all her debts."

"Then why does the bank want to foreclose? You said yourself they'll be losing money."

"They will, but they're trying to cut their losses. They don't want to lose any more money than they already have." He gave her a sympathetic look. "I'm sorry, honey, but it can be a cold world out there."

Meg stopped pacing and stared down at him. "There are other banks," she said defiantly. "If necessary, I'll apply for the loan myself."

"I don't think that will help. Chefs aren't exactly the highest-paid profession in Houston."

"There must be something I can do. I can't just stand by and see everything they worked for go down the drain," she cried in frustration.

"I thought you'd feel that way. That's why I stopped by. I have a business proposition for you."

Meg sank down in her chair and leaned forward eagerly. "What is it?"

"I'll see to it that she gets the loan."

"How?" Meg wanted to know. "I thought you said she has no collateral."

"She has no collateral that would interest a bank. But

she has one piece of collateral that interests me very much."

Meg frowned. "What's that?"

He gave her a slightly wicked grin. "You."

Meg felt the color flood her face. "I don't understand," she stammered.

"It's quite simple. I'll see that Helen gets her money, and in return you move out to Broken Rock with me. My cook just quit, and I need someone to take her place."

Meg stared at him in confusion. He wasn't making much sense. There were easier ways to go about getting a cook.

"What is it you really want?" she asked suspiciously.

This time as he looked at her, his eyes danced. "You," he said again. "I want you."

Meg was shocked into speechlessness.

"Seven years ago, if you had been older, we could have had something pretty special. I told you that one day I'd want to finish what we started that night down by the creek, and that day has come."

"What about what I want?" Meg asked angrily. "Hasn't it occurred to you that I may not be interested in you anymore?"

He lifted his shoulders nonchalantly. "I think you want exactly what I want. You're just not willing to admit it."

"I have no intention of moving out to Broken Rock to become your live-in plaything," she told him in cold tones. She was so angry she could barely speak. "I'm surprised you have the nerve to suggest such a thing."

"I'm not suggesting it," he pointed out, "although I don't think it's such a bad idea. You're the one who is jumping to conclusions. All I'm asking you to do is cook for my men."

Meg was getting confused. "But you just said—" Her voice faltered.

"I said I want you. I do. But I'm not going to force

you. Once you're at Broken Rock, I'm willing to let nature take its course."

"You're very confident, aren't you?" she asked bitterly.

"Not without cause. Surely you haven't forgotten what we shared that night. You weren't experienced enough to realize it, but it was special—and it can be again."

Meg felt the color mount to her face once more. "You're crazy," she said. "I'm not interested in picking up where we left off." She changed tactics suddenly. "Can't you see to it that Aunt Helen gets the money without all this? I'll pay you back, I promise."

"Sorry, honey," he said in that slow, lazy drawl of his. "I'm a businessman, just like the banks. I want collateral. And you're the only collateral I'll accept."

She stared at him wishing she could throw him out. But she didn't dare. He might be the only thing to stand between her aunt and heartbreak.

"You said you owed my uncle a great deal," she reminded him.

"And I also said I more than paid him back," he said harshly. His voice softened a little. "Besides, your aunt wouldn't want any favors."

"She wouldn't want me to sell myself to save the ranch, either," Meg countered.

"I'm not asking you to sell yourself," he said mildly. "I'm asking you to sell your services as a chef. I don't want to buy your body. I want it to be freely given. When you come to me, I want it to be because you want to, not for any other reason."

"Let me get this straight," she said. She was trying not to let what she saw in his eyes confuse her. "If I agree to move out to Broken Rock and cook for your hands, you'll see to it that my aunt gets her loan. Is that it?"

"That's it."

"How long do you expect me to stay there?"

He gave her a considering look. "Let's say three months."

"Three months," she repeated. "And there's nothing else to it?"

"It's just a simple business deal," he told her. "Although I hope it will turn into something more."

"And when it doesn't?" she asked dangerously.

He shrugged as though he didn't believe that were possible. "Then you've helped your aunt save her ranch, and I've gotten a good cook."

Meg got up and walked over to the windows so that he couldn't see her face. His eyes followed her as she stared at the twinkling lights of Houston.

"The whole thing is ridiculous," she said. "I can't just walk away from my job, from everything I've worked so hard to achieve. Besides, what would people think if I moved out to your ranch?"

"I don't care what people think," he answered with angry impatience.

She swung around and looked at him. "You may not care what people think," she said quietly, "but I do."

He made an effort to speak more reasonably. "If people think anything, they'll probably think it's nice of you to move out to Broken Rock where you can be closer to your aunt. As for my men, they'll be delighted to get some real food again. They're taking turns doing the cooking now, and they're almost starving."

He got up and walked over to her. As he got closer, Meg had to keep herself from stepping backward. She didn't want him to think she was afraid. Clay stopped just in front of her and cupped her chin with his hand.

"You won't regret coming," he told her softly. "I can promise you that."

"You're very sure of yourself," Meg said. A certain breathlessness robbed her words of their sting.

His eyes probed hers. "I try to be," he said lightly.

He bent over and kissed her. As soon as their lips met, he pulled her into his arms. His passion ignited an immediate response in Meg. After seven years, it was heaven to be in his arms again. She relaxed against him, her body threatening to betray her as she gave herself to him without a thought of protest.

"I didn't think it would be like that," she whispered unsteadily.

"I did," Clay muttered hoarsely. "Seven years is a long time, but I haven't forgotten what it was like between us."

Meg tried to twist away from him. The look in his eyes frightened her. "That's silly." Her voice trembled as she spoke. "I'm just another woman."

"You're not just another woman," he told her harshly. "Feel my heart." He pressed her hand against his chest. "Other women don't do that to me."

Meg stared up at him dazedly. His heart was thundering under her hand.

"That's what you do to me," he said softly. His eyes were dark, molten pools. "And I'll bet anything your heart is pounding just as hard."

She shook her head. "No," she said weakly.

He put his hand over her heart, and Meg gasped at the intimate contact.

"I'm right," he said firmly. "It's still there. After all these years, it's still there. Come to the ranch," he urged her. "We'll make magic together, Meg. I promise you."

Meg stared back at him. She was trying not to be carried along by his mood.

He began kissing her cheek, her ear, her neck. "For seven years I've thought of what it would be like to make love to you. For seven years I've remembered that night by the river and the way you—"

With a strange little cry, Meg jerked away. "I don't want this," she cried out.

His eyes watched her steadily, although he made no move to take her back in his arms.

"I think you do," he told her quietly. "I know I do." His voice suddenly turned impatient. "Well, what do you say? Are you going to accept my offer and move out to Broken Rock?"

She pushed back her hair with a trembling hand. "I don't know," she told him. "I need time to think about it." Her voice grew stronger. "But if I do, it will be a business arrangement and nothing else. I don't feel anything for you anymore."

His dark eyes glittered. "You don't feel anything for me anymore," he repeated mockingly. "Your face is flushed, your lips are swollen, and your heart is racing. Someone should tell your body that."

"I want you to leave," Meg said as steadily as she could. "I'll call you and let you know what I've decided."

"Don't take too long," he warned her. "I've waited for you long enough."

Meg stared at the door after he had closed it behind him and tried to gain control of her emotions. She felt as though she were fighting her way through an invisible web of passion.

CHAPTER THREE

Meg opened her eyes to find herself in the familiar room of her childhood. She stretched languorously, then snuggled down into the soft bed for a few more minutes of sleep. The last few weeks had been hectic, and she was worn out.

Henry had refused to accept the fact that Meg wouldn't marry him. She had tried to let him down gently, perhaps too gently, she thought now. He had offered her time to "find herself," time to discover what she really wanted out of life. But he would be in touch, he promised, much to her annoyance.

Everyone else had been wonderful. The powers that be at her TV station had decided they could rerun her old shows over the summer, giving her some breathing space. Jake Rhinehart, too, refused to consider her departure as anything more than a leave of absence. Meg was delighted. That meant she would have a job to return to once Clay no longer required her as collateral for his loan.

She blushed as she thought of Clay. Although she hadn't seen him since that night when he had come to her apartment, he hadn't been far from her thoughts. She knew she was walking into the lion's den, but what else could she do? There was no way she could turn her back on her aunt, and Clay had known that when he made his proposition.

The door to Meg's room opened, and Helen came in with a tray.

"I thought you might like breakfast in bed," she said.

"That sounds heavenly," Meg told her. "But you shouldn't spoil me like this."

"I enjoy spoiling you," Helen replied. Her voice softened. "You couldn't mean more to me if you were my own daughter. Besides, you look like you could use some spoiling. You work too hard in the city, and you certainly won't be spoiled over at Broken Rock."

Meg laughed. "I'm sure that's true."

"I still don't understand why you're going to work for Clay," Helen went on.

"I told you last night," Meg said patiently. She had repeated this story to herself so many times, she almost believed it was the truth—almost. "For several months, I've wanted to write a cookbook, but I've been too busy to get started on it. When I heard Clay was looking for a cook, it sounded ideal. At Broken Rock, I'll have more time, and I can feed my experiments to his hands."

Helen laughed.

"Besides," Meg added, "I like the idea of being closer to you for a while."

"I'm not going to quarrel with that," Helen said promptly. "Having you at Broken Rock is the next best thing to having you here."

Meg poured her aunt a cup of coffee, and Helen sat down on the chair across from the bed to drink it.

"As a matter of fact," Helen said casually, "things are going to be changing here, too."

"Oh?" Meg asked curiously. "How?" From a phone conversation with Clay, she knew the bank loan had been approved. Her aunt, though, had never mentioned it, and neither had Meg. She didn't want Helen to know the part she played in the approval of the loan.

"I've hired some new men to help me out," Helen told her. "They'll be starting in the next couple of days."

"That's great."

Helen nodded. "The fact is, the ranch has been a little too much for me since your uncle died, and when Clay offered me the use of some of his men, I didn't think I could refuse."

Meg put down her coffee cup. "Clay offered you the use of some of his men?"

"I'm paying him for their time, of course," Helen told her quickly. "He said he was cutting back and didn't have enough work for all of them this year, but he hated to let them go because they're such good men. So we worked out a deal."

"I hope he's not charging you some outrageous sum," Meg said suspiciously.

"You know better than that," Helen said reprovingly. "As a matter of fact, he's charging me far less than he should. I don't know what I would have done without Clay since your uncle's death. He's been wonderful."

"He thinks a lot of you," Meg told her gently, "and Uncle John was like a father to him."

Helen nodded. "I know. I just wish—" She gave Meg a strange look, then changed the subject. "What time are you going over to Broken Rock?"

"Right after breakfast," Meg replied. "I promised Clay I'd be there in time to fix lunch."

Helen glanced at the clock. "You'd better get going, then." She got up and moved the breakfast tray from Meg's lap.

"You're right," Meg said. "I have a feeling it's going to take days to get the kitchen straightened out. They've been on their own over there for nearly a month now."

Helen laughed. "Then the sooner you get going, the sooner you'll be finished."

It wasn't going to take days, it was going to take weeks, Meg thought as she looked around the kitchen in consternation. There were dirty dishes in the sink, and the stove looked as though it hadn't been cleaned in a year.

She dropped her suitcase just inside the door, then immediately set to work. By lunchtime, she had the dishes done, but she knew it would take the rest of the day to get the kitchen back to normal.

Clay wasn't there for lunch, which was just as well as far as Meg was concerned. She fed the men a hastily thrown together casserole of meat, beans, and rice, which they seemed to enjoy.

It wasn't until Meg had cleaned out the refrigerator, scrubbed the floor, and washed the counters and cabinets that Clay appeared.

"Working hard?" he asked.

Meg turned around to face him with a sinking heart. She always managed to look her worst around him. She was wearing a pair of cutoff jeans and a T-shirt that had been clean at the beginning of the day but was now filthy. She had tied her hair back with a scarf, but strands were escaping in all directions.

Clay, on the other hand, looked fantastic. His faded blue jeans and partially unbuttoned Western-cut shirt suited his long, loose-limbed body to perfection.

"How in the world did this kitchen get so dirty?" she asked. She forced her eyes away from the dark, curling hair on his chest. Looking into his face was even worse, she decided. His dark eyes were taking in every aspect of her appearance.

He ignored her question. "The men are delighted to have you here," he said. "They're already telling me what a good cook you are." His eyes narrowed as they moved slowly down her body. "I'm glad to have you here, too, honey," he drawled as his gaze reluctantly ceased its exploration. "Though not for the same reason."

She dragged her eyes from his. "I think the kitchen looks very nice now that I've cleaned it," she said brightly. "Don't you?"

"You're what looks nice to me," he replied. "Broken Rock is sorely in need of a woman's touch, and so am I." His eyes blazed suddenly and he came toward her. "Meg," he began in an anguished voice.

The look on his face frightened her a little. It was as though a mask had been stripped away, revealing an almost desperate determination. She couldn't help feeling alarmed.

"Don't, Clay," she said as he reached for her. She hoped she didn't sound as panic-stricken as she felt.

"Why the hell not?" he asked. "This is where you belong." His hands closed over her arms, and he began pulling her to him.

"You said you wouldn't push me."

"I said I wouldn't force you into doing anything you don't want to do," he interrupted. "I didn't say I wouldn't push a little. There's a difference."

"Not in my book," she said sharply. "Besides, I probably smell like ammonia."

He looked down at her quizzically. "If that's all that's bothering you," he said just before he kissed her.

Meg felt her knees grow weak, and she tried to resist the force of his kiss, but the strength of his arms was overpowering. Resistance was useless, and she knew it.

"You may smell like ammonia," he told her a moment later, "but you taste like honey."

His lips found hers again, and this time Meg's arms went around his neck and her fingers moved gently through his thick black hair. Finally, she took her lips from his.

"Let me go."

"No," he muttered. "Not yet. I've waited too long to hold you in my arms."

"I've got to prepare dinner for your men, and I need a shower," she said, trying to force herself from his powerful arms.

"After dinner—" he began.

"After dinner, we'll talk. Please, Clay, let me go." At last he did as she asked. "Now, where am I going to sleep?" she asked, her voice a bit shaky.

That brought a half-smile to his face. "Upstairs," he told her.

"Upstairs?" she echoed, with obvious dismay.

"Where else would you sleep?" he asked reasonably. "I can't exactly put you out in the bunkhouse with the men."

"No, of course not," she agreed impatiently. "But where did your cook sleep? Didn't she have separate quarters off the kitchen?"

"She did, but I've had to turn that into a temporary storage area. You wouldn't be comfortable there. The room is full of boxes."

She'd be a lot more comfortable there than upstairs with Clay only a few feet away.

"You don't need to be afraid," he said softly, as if he'd read her mind. "If it makes you feel better, there's a lock on your door, although there won't be any reason for you to use it. I won't go into your room until you invite me."

Meg's face flushed, but she spoke with bravado that she didn't feel. "In that case, everything should be all right. Just show me to my room."

He picked up her suitcase and led the way out of the kitchen. In the hall, however, he waited until she could catch up to him, then draped his arm around her shoulder. His touch was far more than companionable, Meg thought as she felt the strength and power in his arm. All the way up the wide staircase, she chattered brightly and

48

as impersonally as she could about the beauty of his home.

After the men had eaten in a small room off the kitchen, Meg and Clay sat down to their own dinner in the dining room. Although she would have rather eaten with the men, Clay insisted on doing it this way.

"You're here to cook for the men, not to entertain them," he had growled when Meg protested at the arrangements. "During the day, you can cook for them, but in the evenings, you're mine."

In spite of her nervousness and her determination to keep Clay at a distance, Meg had been strangely flattered. Against her better judgment, she had given in to his wishes.

All during the meal, though, she wished she hadn't. There should have been nothing at all romantic about their dinner, but somehow Clay managed to give it an intimate feel. Perhaps it was the way he looked at her. She had removed the candles from the table, and the lights were bright rather than dim. There was nothing in the meal itself to inspire romance, either. She had prepared a meat loaf, the only thing the depleted pantry would allow, which she served with green beans and glasses of icy-cold milk. It was an ordinary meal served in a brightly lit room, and yet Meg had the feeling that she was in a dark, intimate restaurant where she and Clay had nothing to do but savor the food and wine and each other. The way he gazed at her across the table did nothing to dispel that feeling either. Meg looked up time and time again, determined to discuss the weather or something equally impersonal. Each time, she found her blue eyes trapped by Clay's silver ones until she felt she would drown in their depths. She forgot about everything but the two of them and the trembling excitement that seemed to be flowing back and forth across the table.

This was how it would be if we were married, Meg told herself as they talked about day-to-day things. At that thought, something twisted inside her. Clay hadn't wanted her love seven years ago. Now he'd made it clear he wanted her body, and that wasn't the same thing.

"That wasn't a speciality from La Bonne Femme, but is sure tasted good," he told her as she got up to clear the table.

"I'm afraid it wasn't much of a feast," she said apologetically.

His hand closed over her arm, and she reached for his plate. "It's not the food I'm interested in," he said softly.

"Do you want some coffee?" she asked steadily, although her pulse was suddenly racing.

"You know what I want," he persisted in a dark voice. "I want you."

"I'm not available, and the coffee is," she replied as flippantly as she could. She pulled her arms free. "I'll bring it to the living room in a few moments."

She fled into the kitchen wondering how she was ever going to get through the next three months. By the time the coffee was ready, she felt a little calmer. She took it out to him, determined to make him understand her feelings once and for all.

"I want to thank you for everything you've done for my aunt," she told him a few minutes later. She had found him outside on the terrace instead of in the living room.

"I haven't done anything," he replied brusquely.

"You sent some of your men over to help her," she retorted. "I'd hardly call that nothing." She poured him a cup of coffee and placed it near his hand.

"She needs them and I don't."

"Nevertheless, it was kind of you to think of it. I'm very grateful."

"Are you?" he asked. The coldness had left his voice. "Would you like to come over here and show me just how grateful you are?"

"No, I wouldn't," she said, sitting down in a chair just out of his reach.

"Who are you afraid of?" he asked. "Me or yourself?"

There was a seductive note to his voice that Meg decided to ignore.

"It's not that I'm afraid," she told him. "Not in the way you mean it." She took a deep breath. "I want you to understand how I feel, Clay," she went on earnestly. "Seven years ago you hurt me. I don't want to be hurt again."

"I couldn't have hurt you much," he said darkly. "You forgot all about me as soon as you got back to college."

She shrugged. "You made your feelings very clear that night, and after a while I grew out of my crush on you."

"Then what makes you think I could hurt you again?" he asked.

"In any kind of affair, there's a risk of being hurt," Meg said with a calmness she didn't feel.

"Oh?" Clay asked. He got up and walked to the edge of the terrace. When he turned back to face her, Meg could see his eyes glitter. "I didn't realize you were an expert in affairs."

"I don't need expert knowledge to know that," she said. "Just a little common sense." She leaned forward. "Try to understand how I feel, Clay," she said urgently. "At twelve, I idolized you. At eighteen, I had a crush on you. But all that has changed. I've grown up. Now you're a friend. Nothing more."

"Before you go back to Houston, I'm going to be much more than that."

"No," she said, although she was beginning to tremble. He sounded so sure of himself.

"Yes," he said softly.

In two strides, he was standing in front of her. Before Meg realized what was happening, he had pulled her out of her chair.

"If I took you in my arms right now and kissed you, I

could make you kiss me back," he told her. "I could make you want me." His hands tightened on her shoulders.

"You said you wouldn't force me," Meg reminded him breathlessly.

"I may be changing my mind about that. Perhaps a little forcing is just what you need." He ran a finger along her jawline, then cupped her chin in his hand. "Look at me, Meg, and tell me you don't want to make love to me," he demanded quietly.

Meg got hold herself and looked up at him. "I don't want to make love to you," she said as steadily as she could. She knew he would never believe her if he sensed the panic that was racing through her.

"You're a good liar," he told her. "But I don't believe you. And this is why."

He kissed her once with a tantalizing lightness, then again. The second time, their lips clung together and Meg felt his arms go around her hungrily. Instinctively, she responded. Her arms circled his neck, and she went up on tiptoe so she could press her body against his. For a moment she gave herself to the kiss, matching his passion with an answering passion of her own. For a moment her body ached for something deeper, more fulfilling. Then, feeling suddenly embarrassed and more than a little shaken, she tried to pull away.

That wasn't the way to make Clay think she wasn't interested in him, she thought impatiently.

"You can't deny that reaction," Clay told her.

She didn't try to. He was right. She couldn't deny the way she responded to him. Even if she did, he wouldn't believe it.

"We could be very good together," he murmured. His arms were still around her. "Give in to your feelings," he urged her. "You'll be glad you did."

She pulled herself free. "It's too late for that."

"You were willing once," he told her. "I can remember when you asked me to make love to you."

Her face burned in the darkness. "I was very young," she answered. "I had a schoolgirl crush on you."

"You were no schoolgirl when you put your arms around me and asked me to teach you about love. If I had it to do over again, that evening would end very differently."

He was suddenly so angry that Meg took a step backward.

"I should have taken you then and there. I should have made love to you, Meg. If I had, we wouldn't be playing these games today."

"I would have hated you for it," Meg told him.

His anger disappeared as quickly as it had come. "Would you? I don't believe that."

She was beginning to feel a little desperate. "None of that matters anymore," she said. "That's all in the past. You've got to realize, Clay, that what I felt for you then doesn't give you the right to my body anytime you choose to claim it."

CHAPTER FOUR

"Rise and shine, honey," Clay called from the other side of Meg's bedroom door.

She opened one eye, glanced at the clock and groaned. It was five forty-five. She'd almost forgotten how early a day on the ranch started.

I hope Clay isn't going to make a habit of personally waking me, she thought as she sat up.

Then she heard the doorknob turn, and she hurriedly pulled the sheets up to her neck as Clay's head popped around the door. She stared at him indignantly, but he didn't seem to notice.

"If you hurry and get dressed, we'll have time to go riding before breakfast." Before she could answer, his head disappeared and he closed the door softly behind him.

Meg got up and dressed quickly. It was, she told herself firmly, the prospect of riding around Broken Rock that appealed to her, not the idea of spending time with Clay. She hadn't seen the ranch in seven years, and she was anxious to see what changes he had made.

Clay was waiting for her in the kitchen. His eyes slid over her approvingly as she appeared in the doorway. She was wearing tight jeans and a short-sleeved plaid shirt that brought out the color of her soft blue eyes. He poured a cup of hot, steaming coffee and held it out to her.

"I'm supposed to be the cook," she said as she reached for the cup. She was careful not to let her fingers graze his as she took it. "I should have made the coffee for you."

"You can make it for me tomorrow morning," he returned easily. "And it won't hurt the men to have to wait for their breakfast. Now, how about that ride?"

Meg took a few hurried sips of coffee, then followed him out to the barn.

"I haven't been on a horse in nearly a year," she said ruefully as she stared at the sleek animal Clay had picked out for her to ride. The two of them were standing alone in the paddock area off to the side of the barn. "I'll probably be too sore to move tomorrow."

"I know just how to take care of that," Clay said immediately. "I've got some lotions that work wonders. I'll even rub them on for you," he offered in a blatantly sensual tone.

"No, thank you," Meg replied primly as she moved toward her horse. "I think I can manage that for myself."

She stopped and watched as Clay swung himself up into the saddle. He moved with the easy grace of a man who knew the strength of his own body. He was more than just good-looking, she thought as her eyes ranged over his face.

He looked down, caught her staring, and gave her a wink. Meg blushed slightly.

"I want to talk to Bill a minute," he told her. "Can you manage on your own?"

"I've been riding horses since I was three," she reminded him sharply. Without another look, she walked purposefully to the spot where her horse was standing.

"That's a mighty big horse for a pretty little thing like you," a lazy voice said close behind her.

Meg jumped slightly and moved forward a few steps. Standing behind her was Wild Whip Hawkins, one of Clay's more disreputable hands. He seemed to have materialized out of nowhere. She laughed a little nervously. There was something in Whip's eyes that she didn't like.

"He is big, isn't he?" she agreed lightly.

"You'd better let me give you a leg up, ma'am," Whip said. On the surface, his colorless voice was perfectly respectful and his face reflected only friendly concern, but there was something about him that made Meg uncomfortable.

"Thanks, but I can manage by myself," she said coolly. She turned away dismissively.

"It's no trouble," Whip told her. He moved a step closer and took hold of her elbow. Meg flinched and tried to shake him off. "I wouldn't want to see someone as pretty as you get hurt."

"What's going on here?" Clay asked. He had come riding over as soon as he noticed Whip at Meg's elbow. His face was thunderous.

"I was just offering the lady a leg up, boss," Whip said. He plaited his fingers and held out his hands so that Meg could step into them.

Meg started to refuse again, but a quick glance at Clay's face convinced her it would be better to let Whip help her. Clay was obviously annoyed by Whip's attention, and she didn't want to draw out the scene any longer. So she let Whip help her up, then thanked him coolly before she turned to give Clay a smile.

"Ready?" she asked.

He smiled back, and the cloud lifted from his face for a moment. Then he turned back to Whip, and his eyes were icy.

"Bill needs some help with that piece of fence that came down the other day," he said coldly.

"Okay, boss," Whip replied tonelessly. He ambled off without another look at Meg.

Clay watched him go, then turned back to Meg. He looked worried. "I want you to stay away from Whip," he told her. "He's a good cowhand, but his reputation with women is known all over."

"I gathered as much from his name," Meg said dryly. She'd gladly keep away from Wild Whip Hawkins.

Clay wheeled his horse around, and they headed out toward the pasture. His posture was faultless, and there was confidence in every line of his body, Meg noticed as she glanced over at him.

"Does it look any different?" he asked as they rode companionably along the gleaming white fence that separated one pasture from another.

"Not really," she returned. "There's a timelessness about a place like this. I always did say that this was the nicest ranch in Texas, except for my aunt's, of course," she teased.

He grinned back. "Of course," he said. "I've got to go into town for a board meeting today. What are you going to be doing?"

"After breakfast, I'm going to make a list of all the things I need. Then this afternoon, Aunt Helen is stopping by, and we're going into Morganville to do some shopping. It's going to be an expensive afternoon," she warned him. "I've never seen such a depleted pantry."

Clay shrugged indifferently. "I've got accounts at all the major stores. Get whatever you think you need."

"Oh, I will," she told him. "Don't worry about that. I'll be ordering some things from Houston, too. I'm afraid you're going to find that I'm considerably more expensive than your last cook. You may not think I'm worth it."

Clay turned warm eyes on her face. "I doubt that," he said simply. They stared at each other for a long moment until Meg was finally able to tear her eyes away. She was surprised to find that her heart was suddenly racing.

"What do you need from Houston that you can't get in Morganville?" Clay asked.

"Some exotic Indian spices, gold foil," Meg said mischievously. "Things like that."

"The men like simple food," Clay warned her.

"Well, they're not going to get it. I'm going to do some experimenting while I'm here, and you and your men are going to be my guinea pigs."

"Just don't get too fancy," he said, "or I'll have a mutiny on my hands."

"Oh, they'll like what I serve them. I think I can promise you that."

"Why all the experimenting?" he wanted to know.

"I'm going to write a cookbook," she told him. "I thought I'd put the time I'm here to good use."

Clay shot her a dark look. "If you'd stop being so damned stubborn, we could put the time to very good use." His voice was so pregnant with meaning that Meg felt herself blush.

"Really, Clay," she burst out a little angrily. "Don't you ever think of anything but sex?"

"Who says I'm thinking of sex?" he returned surprisingly. "When I think of you, I think of lovemaking, not sex."

"They're the same thing," she said shortly.

"That's where you're wrong. Sex is an impersonal, purely physical act. I want more than that with you. I want us to make love, to explore each other's bodies and minds. I want to know you in every way, and I want you to know me intimately, too."

"I don't want to know you intimately," Meg said a little crossly. She didn't like the direction this conversation was going.

Clay moved his horse in close, reached over, took the reins, and brought both horses to a stop. "It won't do you

58

any good to run from what there is between us," he said deliberately. "I'll find you wherever you try to hide."

"How many times do I have to tell you, there is nothing between us except some kind of physical attraction that exists only in your mind?" Meg asked in exasperation.

Clay shook his head. "You don't really believe that." His voice grew more persuasive. "Believe me, Meg, if all I wanted was sex, you would have been mine by now."

She started to protest, but Clay ignored her.

"I want more than an affair. I want something lasting, I want it to mean something to both of us."

Almost unwillingly, Meg looked at him. His eyes burned into hers, and she felt strangely breathless.

"I think we'd better get back," she said, looking everywhere but at him. "It's getting late, and the men are probably hungry."

Clay chuckled softly, but he obediently let go of her reins.

"I'm glad Helen is stopping by this afternoon," he said as they retraced their steps. "It's good for her to have you so close by. She needs you. We both do."

Meg forced herself to harden her heart. Clay might think he needed her, but it obviously wasn't in any kind of meaningful way. He could play all the semantics games he wanted, but it was still her body he was interested in and nothing else.

"Hey, boss," one of the men called as they rode in.

"I'll go see what he wants," Clay told her as she dismounted.

She nodded coolly. She was angry, upset, and confused. "I'll stable the horse, then go start breakfast." Without another word, she led her horse into the barn.

He made everything sound so plausible, she thought resentfully to herself as she began to rub down the horse. He wanted her, and he meant to have her.

"Did you have a good ride?" Wild Whip asked. She hadn't realized it, but he had followed her into the stable.

"Very nice, thank you," Meg said uneasily. She gave the horse a final pat, then turned and took a step toward the door. Whip blocked the way.

"What's your hurry?" he asked, his voice slightly menacing.

"I've got breakfast to prepare," Meg said, trying to sound calm. She cast a glance over his shoulder. The door suddenly seemed a long way off.

"I thought you and me ought to get to know one another," Whip murmured. He took a step toward her, and Meg realized that he had no intention of letting her leave. He reached out and touched her hair.

Meg pushed his hands away. "Let me by this instant," she said icily.

He ignored her. "You're mighty pretty," he said. He moved even closer.

"If you touch me again, I'll scream," Meg told him. She managed to keep her voice steady, although she wasn't sure how she did it. Her alarm had turned to fear, and her fear was rapidly turning to panic. She shrank back against the rough boards of the horse's stall.

"There ain't nobody to hear you," he replied. "The boss and Pete rode off a few minutes ago. That gives us a little time to get acquainted."

He put his hand on her arm, and Meg screamed. The next few seconds passed in a blur. She was aware of Whip trying to kiss her, then suddenly he was lying sprawled on his back in the dust and Clay was standing over him.

"Did he hurt you?" Clay asked her. His face was terrible to see. It might have been carved out of granite.

Meg shook her head. "There wasn't time," she said a little incoherently. Her knees were beginning to shake. She put her hand on the stall for support.

Clay looked down at Whip. He was sitting up now, nursing his jaw. "It's a good thing for you that I came back," he told the other man in a tone that was colder than ice. His eyes were blazing silver. "If you'd hurt her, I'd have torn you apart with my bare hands. As it is, you're fired. Gather up your belongings and be off the ranch in fifteen minutes."

Whip took one look at Clay, got to his feet, and made his way toward the door. Clay watched him go, then turned to Meg.

"Are you sure he didn't hurt you?" he asked anxiously. The rigid lines of his face eased as he looked at her.

"He just frightened me," Meg said shakily. "If you hadn't come back—" She shuddered. "He told me you had ridden off. What made you come back?"

"God knows," he replied simply. "I must have some kind of special radar working where you're concerned." His voice changed abruptly. "I thought I told you to stay away from Whip," he said sharply. "What were you doing in here with him, anyway?"

Meg was taken aback by the unfairness of Clay's attack. "I didn't entice him in here, if that's what you're thinking," she said angrily. "He followed me, and when I tried to leave, he wouldn't let me." She shook again as she remembered the look on Wild Whip's face.

Clay saw the convulsive movement of her shoulders, and his voice softened. "I'm sorry," he said. Gently he pulled her to him, and Meg leaned against him, needing the safety of his arms. "I know it wasn't your fault. The fact is that I can't stand the idea of another man, any man, touching you. When I think of that man your aunt told me about, when I think about all the men who have been in your life the past seven years, I go a little crazy."

Meg looked up at him, and something in his face pulled at her heartstrings. She felt an absurd desire to reassure him. It was so strong that it overrode the confusion she had felt earlier.

"There haven't been a lot of men in my life," she said quietly.

"What about that man who asked you to marry him?" Clay asked above her. "He must have been a large part of your life."

"Yes, he was, but not in the way you mean. He—We."

Clay seemed to grow still all over. With her body touching his, Meg could feel a quietness about him that she had never noticed before.

"Are you trying to tell me that you're a virgin?" he asked. He sounded as though he didn't quite believe what he was hearing.

Meg stiffened. "You needn't make it sound so terrible."

He looked down at her, and there was a new tenderness in his eyes.

"It isn't terrible, it's wonderful. My little Meg," he said, giving her his crooked smile. "I'll make you so glad you waited for me."

"I didn't wait for you," she said angrily. She pulled away abruptly. Reaction was setting in, and she was sorry she had told Clay anything, sorry she had given in to the urge to comfort him. More confused than ever, she pulled away, walked around him, and hurried toward the house.

"There's a dance in Morganville tonight," Jimmy Smith told her a little shyly as he finished his lunch. Jimmy was eighteen and the youngest of Clay's men. He was the last one to eat, and they were alone in the kitchen.

"Oh, what kind of a dance?" Meg asked. She poured herself a glass of iced tea and sat down across the table from him. She liked Jimmy. He was a thoughtful, considerate boy who was spending the summer working for Clay to earn money for college.

"It's an old-fashioned square dance," he told her.

"That sounds like fun," she said a little wistfully. "I haven't been to a square dance in years."

"I'm going with some of the guys. If you're not busy, why don't you come along?"

"I'd like that," she told him, and she meant it. She'd been at Broken Rock for over a week, and she hadn't had any time to herself. "But I'll have to check with Clay first. He may need me here."

"Check with me about what?" Clay asked as he strode into the kitchen and tossed his suitcoat over the back of a chair. He had just gotten back from Houston, and he looked hot and irritable. He was dressed in a conservative gray suit, with a white shirt and a maroon silk tie. With one hand he opened the refrigerator and grabbed a can of beer. With his other hand, he yanked off his tie and loosened his tight collar.

"Jimmy was just telling me about the square dance this evening in Morganville," Meg told him. "I thought I'd go if you don't need me here."

"As a matter of fact," he said curtly, "I do need you here tonight."

"I haven't had a night off since I've been here," she reminded him quietly.

He put his beer down on the counter and leaned against it. "You can have next Thursday off," he told her shortly.

"I should hope so," she told him dryly. "That is the Fourth of July, after all. You could hardly keep me chained to the kitchen on Independence Day."

Jimmy looked from Clay to Meg, then got to his feet and carried his plate to the sink. "Thanks for the lunch," he said a little uncertainly as he disappeared through the door.

Clay moved across the kitchen and sat down in the chair Jimmy had just left. Wearily he leaned forward and rested his arms on the table. "I don't want you going out with the men, Meg. So just leave it alone."

"Did you have a bad morning?" Meg asked. He looked worn out.

"You could say that. A successful company doesn't run itself."

"Not even a successful oil company?" Meg teased gently. "I thought all you oilmen had to do was sit back and watch the money roll in."

That brought a smile to his face. "I wish it were that easy," he said.

She got up and walked around behind him. "Relax," she commanded softly as she began massaging his shoulders.

"When you touch me," he said a little wryly, "the last thing I want to do is relax."

"Well, try to relax, anyway," she told him. "Don't think about anything for a few minutes, and I promise you'll feel better."

Clay was silent as she smoothed the knots out of his tense muscles. Meg moved her hands over his broad shoulders a little shyly at first, then with more confidence as she felt the kinks disappear.

Then, with swiftness that startled her, he turned and buried his face in her breast. His arms circled her waist, and he held her close. For a moment or two, Meg let herself enjoy the contact. Then she removed his arms and stepped back.

"Did you have lunch in town?" she asked in her best cook's voice. She was trying to ignore the way his touch quickened her pulse.

"No," he said. "I was so disgusted that I just wanted to get back to the ranch."

"No wonder you're tense and irritable," she told him as she began making him a sandwich. "You're probably hungry."

"I'm hungry, all right," Clay said softly. "But not for food."

The tone of his voice made her hands tremble as she cut his sandwich in half and put it on a plate.

"Meg," he commanded. "Turn around and look at me."

Meg did as he asked. She was holding the plate in her hands, and the sandwich sitting on it shook dangerously.

"I'm hungry for something only you can give me," he told her. His eyes searched hers. "How much longer are you going to ask me to wait?"

Meg stared back at him. His frustration and desire for her were so apparent that she felt her heart begin to pound against her ribs. Clay, staring at her intently, read the confusion and the fear in her face.

"Don't be afraid of me," he told her. "I won't hurt you. I didn't want to hurt you seven years ago, and I don't want to hurt you now."

Meg felt her eyes unexpectedly fill with tears. Clay saw them, too. He stood up suddenly and made a move toward her. The sandwich, which had been clinging precariously to the side of the plate, slid to the floor. Meg bent down and picked it up, blinking back her tears at the same time. Clay hadn't meant to hurt her seven years ago, she told herself, but he had. She had to remember that. The same thing would happen all over again if she weren't careful.

"I'll make you another one," she said when she had wiped the mustard from the floor.

Clay swore softly to himself and sat back down.

"Tell me about your morning," Meg said a few minutes later as she put a second sandwich in front of him. Her voice was casually friendly, and the tears were gone.

"It's the damned government bureaucracy," he said, taking her cue. "They make it almost impossible to get anything done in a reasonable amount of time. I'm not a particularly patient man," he went on, "and I hate wasting time when I could be doing something useful."

No, Meg thought as she listened to him explain the red tape that was currently tying up his latest exploration project, you're not a patient man. She knew that better than anyone.

Early that evening, Meg was standing barefoot in the kitchen, making a salad for dinner. She was dressed in cutoff jeans and a sky blue cotton shirt with a scooped neck and short sleeves. She had pinned her hair up on top of her head, but little tendrils of it had escaped and were curling around her face.

It was hot, Meg thought as she washed the lettuce. In spite of the efficient air conditioning, it was hot. How could it not be when the heat pushed the outside thermometer up over a hundred degrees?

She was tempted to put on her bathing suit and go for a quick swim in the pool behind the house. She'd been tempted to all week long. But she didn't want to expose that much of herself to Clay's intimate scrutiny, and she could never be sure when he'd be popping in.

"Hello, Meg," Clay said behind her. His voice was warm and gently teasing.

Meg turned to find him leaning against the doorjamb, watching her. There was a relaxed grin on his face, and he seemed to have forgotten the troubles he had brought home from the office.

Meg took one look at him and felt her mouth go dry. He was dressed in brief khaki walking shorts that showed off his long, muscular legs to perfection. Meg never knew a man could have such good-looking legs. His cotton shirt stretched across his powerful torso, and tufts of coarse black hair showed at the open collar. He was devastatingly handsome and, what's more, he looked cool and confident. Looking at him, Meg suddenly felt neither. She turned back to the salad, very much aware of the grin on his face.

With a couple of long strides, Clay crossed the kitchen, gathered up the lettuce, dropped it into a bowl, and tossed it casually into the refrigerator.

"Come on," he said, taking her arm and leading her toward the door.

"Where are we going?" she asked. She braced herself for the blast of heat that would hit them once they stepped outside. Much to her surprise, the evening, though not exactly cool, was a pleasant one. The sun was setting slowly, and the sky was streaked with pink.

"Out," Clay said succinctly.

"Out!" she echoed with dismay. "But I can't go out."

"Why not?" he asked reasonably. "All the men have gone to Morganville, and you said yourself it was time you had a night off."

"I know I did, but—" Meg stopped. She couldn't very well tell him she wanted an evening away from him. "I'm not dressed to go anywhere."

Clay's eyes swept over her. "You look pretty good to me," he told her. "Has anyone ever told you that you have sensational legs? And the rest of you isn't bad, either!"

Meg blushed and immediately wished she hadn't. She didn't usually blush easily, but Clay managed to invest his compliments with such intimacy that she couldn't help herself.

"Where are we going?" she asked again as he wrenched open the door of the small pickup truck he sometimes used to ride over the range.

"On a picnic," he replied as he helped her inside the cab of the truck.

As he walked around the front of the truck, Meg watched in consternation. Night was rapidly falling, and the last thing she wanted was to go on a moonlight picnic with Clay. The whole idea was too suggestive, too provocative.

"You said you wanted a night off," he reminded her as he climbed into the car, "and I'm giving it to you."

"I don't trust you," Meg said angrily. "I stayed at the

67

ranch because you said you needed me. I didn't know you were going to kidnap me."

"You can report me to the authorities when we get back," he said imperturbably. He gave her a sidelong glance through the gathering darkness.

Meg was looking around with dismay. The horrible realization was growing within her that Clay was taking her down to the creek where they had spent so many evenings together seven years ago.

"We're going down to the creek," she said, turning accusing eyes on him. There was a note of panic in her voice that she couldn't quite hide.

Clay nodded and gave her a somber look. "I think we need to exorcise some ghosts," he said quietly. There was a steely determination to his voice that Meg had never heard before.

"I don't have any ghosts to exorcise," she said stubbornly.

"Don't you?" he asked softly. "I do."

She sat in silence until they reached the creek. Then she got out of the truck and watched him as he spread a blanket on the ground. Every instinct she possessed urged her to turn and run, if necessary, the two miles or so back to the ranch. Then she got hold of herself. Perhaps he was right, she thought with a tired sigh. Perhaps there were ghosts to deal with.

"Where did you get the food?" she asked as he unpacked a large picnic basket.

"Your aunt fixed it for us," he told her.

"Helen did?" Meg asked in surprise.

"Of course. I told her you were overworked and needed someone to fix dinner for you for a change." He began spooning shrimp salad onto a plate. "She was happy to do it."

He added some french bread and a slice or two of cool melon, then handed her the plate.

"Sit down," he said as she took it. "Unless, of course, you'd rather eat standing up."

Stiffly, Meg sat down on the corner of the blanket. Clay gave her an amused glance but didn't say anything. Instead, he opened the wine and poured and handed her a glass.

"To the future," he said, raising his glass in a toast.

To a future without Clay Beaumont, Meg amended silently as she raised the glass to her lips.

They ate in silence. When they were finished, Clay leaned back and fixed his gaze on her. Darkness had fallen. There was a moon, but it wasn't bright enough yet for her to see his eyes. She wanted to leave, but she knew Clay well enough to know that he wouldn't go until he was ready. So she sat quietly, waiting for him to break the silence.

"I meant what I said when we were driving up here," he said finally. "I think it's time you heard the truth about that night seven years ago."

Meg felt an unexpected surge of bitterness. "I thought you were pretty truthful at the time," she told him. "You let me know in no uncertain terms that I was nothing more than a summer diversion for you."

"I know I hurt you," he responded softly. "But I had to. Can't you see that?"

"No, I can't." Sitting here under the same tall sheltering trees, hearing the same night sounds she had heard before, was bringing back all the pain of that evening. "You didn't have to be so brutal about it. You made me think you wanted me, then you pushed me away."

"I had to," he repeated doggedly. "You were young, you were inexperienced, but you affected me in a way no woman ever had before—and no woman ever has since," he added softly. "If I hadn't been so brutal, as you call it, I wouldn't have been able to restrain myself at all."

Meg pulled her knees up to her chest and wrapped her

arms tightly around them. She *didn't* want to hear this, she *didn't* want to relive that night.

"This isn't going to get us anywhere," she told him coldly. "There's no use that I can see in talking of the past. It's over, and it's been long forgotten."

His anger flared. "It hasn't been forgotten. Every time I look at you, I can see the past in your eyes. It's standing between us." His voice was loud in the stillness of the night.

"That's ridiculous," Meg said weakly. "You're being melodramatic."

"I don't think so," he told her more quietly. "I know you don't want to talk of the past, and after tonight I won't mention it again, if that's what you want. But Meg, why can't you see that I wasn't the ogre you thought I was? I was doing what I thought was best for you."

"Is that what you called it?" Meg asked bitterly. "Is that how you salved your conscience for using me?"

"I didn't use you. I—"

He hesitated for so long that Meg lifted her cheek from her knee and stared at him. Frustration shone from his eyes. He wanted to tell her how her uncle had come to him and persuaded him, against all his instincts, to give Meg time to grow up. He wanted to tell her but, hurt and angry as she was, he was afraid of her reaction.

"I cared for you very much," he said softly. "You claimed you were in love with me. How could I have taken advantage of that?"

Meg stared at him, trying to discover something in his face. Was this the truth, or was there something more?

"You don't seem to mind taking advantage of me now," she pointed out stiffly. "From practically the first minute you walked back into my life, you've been trying to get me into bed with you."

"I admit that." His voice turned earnest. "Seven years ago, you bewitched me. You were all I could think of, and now you've bewitched me all over again. I can't work, I can't sleep. I can't do anything but think of holding you in my arms and loving you."

"Don't say that," Meg cried. "I don't want to hear it. I don't want to hear any of this."

Clay moved forward and rested a large hand on her arm. Meg wanted to pull away, but she couldn't. She was too aware of his strength, his overwhelming masculinity.

"You asked me before to teach you about love," he murmured. "Even though I refused, I wanted to. And I want to even more now. Let me show you, Meg. Let me show you all of the things you've been missing. You won't regret it, I promise."

He moved his hand to her shoulder and gently pulled her to him. She didn't have the strength to resist. His words, his voice, everything about him was so utterly persuasive. He cradled her in his arms for a few sweet seconds before he spoke again.

"Can't you feel how much I need you?" he asked urgently. "Can't you feel every fiber of my being reaching out to you? Just kiss me once, Meg, and you'll understand what I mean."

He tilted her head, and his mouth descended to hers. He meant it to be a gentle kiss, but the moment their lips touched, his passion, and hers too, burst into flames. Clay pulled her against him, and his hands began caressing her feverishly. Meg wrapped her arms around his neck and held him tightly.

"Meg," he muttered in a tortured voice as he buried his face in her neck, "I need you so much. I want you so much I'm about to burn up. Can't you feel my body burning for yours?"

Meg could feel it. She could feel the rigid planes of his body straining toward her as he held her close. She knew his control was beginning to slip away, as hers was also. She wanted Clay even more than she had seven years ago. At that time she had felt the passion of a girl, but now she was experiencing the passion of a woman. In a moment, it would sweep her beyond the boundaries of common sense.

"Give in to it," Clay urged her feverishly. "Give yourself to me, Meg. Now. Tonight."

For a few moments Meg did give in to it. Clay's presence and the touch of his body were so intoxicating that she couldn't help herself. She was aware of everything about him, from the strength of his hands to the feel of his hard body. As he held her close, she could hear the heavy, hard beating of his heart; as his mouth coaxed hers open, she could feel her own heart go wild. Then, with an effort greater than any she had ever made before, she pushed him away.

"I can't," she said miserably. She fought to control her breathing. "I can't." She wanted to, but she was too afraid of the consequences, too afraid of the heartbreak surrender would bring.

"You mean you won't," Clay said flatly.

He hadn't said one word of love, Meg was thinking sadly as she stared blankly past him. He had mentioned everything but love.

And if he had said he loved her? What would she have done then? Meg honestly didn't know. But she did know one thing. She had to guard her heart. She *had* to. People didn't die of broken hearts, not these days. She'd learned that the hard way. But she'd also learned that a broken heart made life scarcely worth living.

Clay rolled over and sat up. Meg immediately stared down at the blanket. She didn't want to look at him. She didn't want to see the anger in his face.

"I'm sorry," he said, much to her surprise. "I didn't mean for that to happen. I brought you down here so we could talk, but when our lips touched, the passion erupted." He leaned forward and spoke more urgently. "There's something between us, Meg. You can't just ignore what we do to each other."

72

Meg didn't answer, and for a few moments there was silence. Then Clay broke it.

"Let's pretend we've just met," he said. Meg could feel the intensity of his gaze on her face, but she still refused to look up. "Let's start over. We'll bury the past once and for all."

"I don't think that will work," Meg said softly. "Too much happened then for us to forget."

"If I can forget," Clay told her roughly, "you certainly can. After all, you were the one who went back to college and immediately got pinned to some fraternity man."

Meg shifted uneasily. Now wasn't the time to tell him that she had made up that fraternity man in a childish attempt to hurt him as much as he had hurt her.

Clay's anger seemed to disappear as quickly as it had come.

"Give me a chance," he said gently. "Give us a chance. That's all I ask. We'll get to know each other all over again. There will be no more talk of the past. From now on, we'll concentrate on the present and the future. I want to know all about you," he told her. "I want to really get to know the woman you've become."

"How?" she asked a little helplessly.

"Well, for starters, you could allow me to escort you to the annual Fourth of July celebration in Morganville next week."

"I'm going with Aunt Helen," she said abruptly.

"Then I'll escort both of you."

Meg shook her head. She didn't want to get to know Clay all over again. She was afraid that if she did, she'd find herself in love again. She was perilously close to being in love with him as it was.

"No. It's simply not a good idea." Though her words were calm, she felt as though she were fighting for her life.

His annoyance erupted into anger. "Why the hell not?" he demanded. He drew an impatient breath.

"We've wasted seven years. Let's not waste any more time." Again he seemed to get hold of his anger. "You've built a wall around yourself," he said more calmly, "and you're hiding behind it."

"That's not true," she said heatedly.

"Then why won't you let me get close to you?" he asked, making it sound like the most reasonable question in the world. "You won't open your mind to me. Or your heart." The last three words seemed to have been dragged out of him.

Meg looked up at him. She was going to tell him once and for all that she would never open her heart to him, that there could never be anything between them. But the words died in her throat. The moon was shining down on them now, and in its light she could see his face clearly. He raised his eyes to hers, and as she saw the bleakness there, she felt herself shiver. His unhappiness was almost tangible. She had to force herself not to reach out to him. Never before, not even the night he had come to her apartment, had Clay shown her so clearly what was behind his sophisticated, urbane manner.

Meg stared at him feeling terribly confused. She knew, no matter how much better it would be for the two of them, that she couldn't reject him completely. Not when he looked at her like that.

Clay was watching her closely. He almost seemed to be following her struggle.

"Can you honestly say you don't have any feeling at all left for me?" he asked her gently. "If you can, tell me now, and I won't bother you again."

"I don't know," Meg whispered. She knew he meant what he said. But now that he had left it up to her, she couldn't banish him from her life.

"Give me a chance," he said softly. "That's all I ask. I'll go as slowly as I can. Just give me a chance." The bleakness in his eyes had been replaced by intensity, urgency.

74

"I can't promise anything." She looked down at the blanket and didn't see the sudden flash of happiness in his eyes.

"You don't have to promise," he assured her. "Just tell me you'll try."

She took a deep breath. "All right," she whispered, "I'll try."

CHAPTER FIVE

The Fourth of July dawned bright and clear and hot. Meg was up early making a chocolate cake for the Women's Club bake sale. Aunt Helen was providing the rest of the lunch—fried chicken, potato salad, watermelon pickles, and, Meg hoped, a big fruit salad. She couldn't help groaning when she thought of all that food, all the calories they would be eating on a day when the temperature promised to top a hundred degrees. However, Clay had always loved her aunt's fried chicken, and Helen loved making it for him.

When the cake—an old-fashioned creation three layers high and filled with a rich fudgey frosting—was finished, Meg changed into the simple halter dress she had decided to wear.

"We're going in style, I see," Meg said from the porch as she watched Clay stow the cake on the backseat of his convertible Cadillac Seville.

"I thought your Aunt would be more comfortable in this than the pickup truck," he answered.

"It's going to be a lovely day," Meg observed as they began the drive into town.

* * *

"It looks nice, doesn't it?" Helen asked as she looked at the bandstand festooned with red, white, and blue streamers and an American flag flying high. A concert was going to be held there that afternoon.

"It's so festive," Meg exclaimed. It had been a long time since she'd been to an old-fashioned Fourth of July celebration.

"You two had better find a spot if you're going to watch the parade," Helen went on. "The sidewalks are filling up fast."

"Aren't you going to watch it with us?" Meg asked in surprise.

Helen shook her head. "I promised to help the ladies from the Women's Club set up for the bake sale. I'll take your cake over for you," she told Meg.

Clay looked at Helen suspiciously. "I thought that cake Meg made was for us."

"It is," Meg told him mischievously. "You just have to buy it back first."

"But I've already paid for the ingredients," he protested, "as well as the time you spent making it. I've been looking forward to eating that cake all morning," he added a little plaintively.

"Don't worry, Clay," Helen told him. "I'll see that it isn't sold to anyone but you. Unfortunately, we'll have to put a high price on it. Since Meg is a celebrity, I'm sure there'll be a great deal of interest in her cake! Now you two run along and find someplace to watch the parade. It should be starting any minute."

"The mayor asked if we'd like to sit in the reviewing stand," Clay told her a few moments later as he swung her up onto the tall stone wall in front of the library. From there they could see over the heads of the people standing in front of them.

Meg almost gasped as his fingers closed around her waist. "That's very flattering," she said once she was

77

seated and Clay had reluctantly removed his hands. "Why are we here instead of there?"

"Because I wanted to be alone with you," Clay said as he effortlessly swung himself up beside her.

"I'd hardly call this being alone," she said as she glanced around her.

"Alone in a crowd," Clay said, giving her his crooked smile. "It's the best I can do." He took her hand in his and held it gently.

A shout went up from the crowd, and a moment later the high school band led by smiling, baton-twirling majorettes started the parade. The band was followed by Miss Independence Day, an excited high school girl riding in a white convertible.

Was I ever that young? Meg wondered to herself. Then the girl caught sight of Clay. She gave him a smile and blew him a big kiss.

"It looks like you've made a conquest," Meg told him.

He merely smiled. "I've already got the woman I want," he said.

Meg looked away and concentrated on the parade. It seemed as though every club and organization for miles around had an entry. There were men on horseback, kids on bicycles, and floats galore. It was, everyone agreed, Morganville's best parade ever.

After lunch, Meg found a spot under a tall old shade tree near the edge of the town square. Clay stretched out beside her and rested his head in her lap. Together they listened to the band as its rousing tunes broke through the hot, still air. Meg closed her eyes and leaned back. Occasionally her fingers moved through Clay's dark, shining hair, but for the most part she was still. It was practically too hot to move.

She was impressed at how well Clay seemed to fit in with his neighbors. That they all knew him came as no surprise to her. Everyone in eastern Texas knew Clay Beaumont. What surprised her was that he knew most of

78

the people he passed on the street—and was genuinely interested in them. In reality, she was thinking, he was quite a bit different from the arrogant, conceited, sophisticated man she had built up in her mind. He could be all those things, of course, she reflected wryly, but he could also be warm, friendly and unassuming.

Dinner was a barbecue sponsored by all the men's clubs in Morganville. Later would come the Fourth of July finale—fireworks that burst brightly over the town.

As they waited for darkness to fall, an impromptu square dance started near the bandstand. Meg listened for a few moments, then got to her feet.

"Where are you going?" Helen asked.

"To watch the square dancing," she replied. "Do either of you want to come?"

"Not me," Clay replied. "It's too hot."

"You wouldn't be so hot if you hadn't eaten all those ribs," Meg told him unsympathetically.

"You go ahead," Helen told her. "Why don't you join in? I'm sure you won't have any trouble finding a partner."

That brought Clay to his feet. "She's already got a partner," he said curtly.

Helen looked over at Meg and winked.

"Can you really square dance?" Meg asked incredulously as they walked toward the bandstand.

"Of course I can," he said, and for the next hour he proved it.

"The fireworks will be starting soon," Helen said when they finally rejoined her. "I promised May Johnson I'd sit with her. She's been trying to talk to me all day, but I've been too busy to listen."

Meg looked at her aunt suspiciously. Since morning, Helen had done her best to throw Meg and Clay together. She had been so successful that Meg had seen practically nothing of her aunt all day long.

Helen smiled back at Meg innocently. "There's May now," she said. With a little wave she hurried away.

Before Meg could say anything, Clay caught her by the hand.

"Come on, I know where we can be alone," he said as he pulled her up the wide library steps.

"That's funny," Meg said lightly, "I was just thinking that we've been alone together most of the day."

"We've been together," he conceded, "but we've hardly been alone. I feel like I've been sharing you with the entire town. Now I want you all to myself."

He led her up the wide library steps and around the side of the building to a spot sheltered by some bushes.

"We won't be able to see the fireworks from here," Meg said. She hung back uncertainly.

Clay gestured up toward the sky. "We'll be able to see them perfectly."

Meg still hung back. The spot was a little too secluded for her. She would have preferred to be where there were more people.

"Have you watched the fireworks from here before?" she asked a little stiffly.

"Are you jealous?" he teased. He took a step toward her and brushed her cheek with his finger. "I've known a lot of women, Meg. Does that bother you?"

"Certainly not," Meg said valiantly. "I've told you before, what you do with your life is your own business."

"And I've told you before that you're not a good enough liar to fool me. The thought of me with another woman bothers you as much as the thought of you with another man bothers me. Why not admit it?"

"Clay," she began helplessly.

She stopped as he reached behind the bushes and pulled out a soft wool blanket.

"What are you doing?" she asked a little blankly.

"Spreading out a blanket," he answered reasonably. "You didn't think I'd expect you to sit on the ground, did you?" He lowered himself onto the blanket and held out his hand to her. Meg ignored it.

"But where did it come from?" she asked instead.

"I put it here earlier," he told her.

"You do think of everything, don't you?"

"I try to," he answered. "Now come and sit down." When she still hesitated, his voice grew teasing. "You don't have anything to worry about," he told her. "I'm hardly going to seduce you here in view of anyone who walks by." He gave her his slightly wicked grin. "You're safe enough—for now."

Again he extended his hand, and this time Meg took it. Clay promptly pulled her down beside him and stretched out beside her.

"When we do make love," he told her as he ran his hand over her hair, "I want it to be very special." His voice thickened a little. "God knows I want you enough to take you here and now, but I won't. We'll wait until everything is right for both of us."

Meg was having trouble breathing. The look on Clay's face both frightened her and drew her closer. She lifted her hand and touched his cheek and Clay leaned over and kissed her. It was a kiss full of aching tenderness, and Meg knew she would never forget it. As their lips met and clung together, a bright golden star burst over them. The fireworks had begun.

"Watch the fireworks," she whispered breathlessly a moment later.

"You watch the fireworks," he told her softly. "I'd rather watch you."

Though Meg did try to watch the fireworks, she found Clay's presence very disturbing. He didn't kiss her again, but his eyes devoured her, and he was constantly touching her face, her hair, her arms.

"Meg," he whispered softly as she stared up at the star-spangled sky, "my sweet Meg."

She turned her head and looked at him, and her resolve to keep him out of her heart weakened. She was just leaning toward him when voices brought her back to earth.

From behind the bushes a girl giggled and the very disappointed voice of a teen-age boy said, "Somebody's already there."

Clay swore softly but not softly enough. The girl giggled again and the boy said, "Come on, I know someplace else we can go."

"So much for privacy," Clay muttered as he sat up. He was irritated, and it showed. "I do my damnedest to get you alone, and when I do, we're practically tripped over by a couple of teen-agers. There goes our romantic moment."

Meg sat up and put her hand on his arm. "It was romantic," she told him tenderly. "In fact, it was probably the most romantic moment of my life."

Clay looked at her, and some of his irritation vanished. "You know how to say the right thing," he said. He was just reaching for her when a rustling sound behind them stopped him.

"It's just around these bushes," a thin, elderly voice said.

As Meg watched, two men and two women, all in their golden years, made their way around the tangle of shrubs. They didn't seem the least bit put out at finding Meg and Clay in the tiny clearing. The man who had been speaking peered at them through the darkness.

"It's Clay Beaumont, isn't it?" he asked. He turned to his companions. "I told you this was a good spot for courting," he said triumphantly. "I used to bring the girls here myself when I was a young fella like you," he told Clay confidentially. "Mind if we join you?" Without waiting for an answer, the four of them sat down on the blanket.

Clay immediately got to his feet and pulled Meg up with him.

"We were just leaving," he said curtly.

"But what about the blanket?" one of the women asked.

"Keep it," Clay threw over his shoulder as he strode toward the library stairs. He held Meg tightly by the hand and was walking so fast that she practically had to run to keep up with him.

"Well, I never," she heard one of the women say as she hurried after Clay.

"Clay!" she protested as she flew behind him down the steep steps to the street. Her hand was still in his. "Slow down."

"We're going to find your aunt and get out of here," he told Meg. He muttered something to himself. Meg only caught the words *Grand Central Station*.

She didn't know how he located Helen in the darkness, but he did. Helen took one look at his face, then cast a questioning look at Meg. Meg raised her shoulders and shook her head. A few moments later, they were on their way out of town.

Once they had dropped Helen off and were on their way back to Broken Rock, Clay began to relax a little.

"I hope you didn't mind missing the last of the fireworks," he told her. It was the first time he had spoken since they had left Morganville.

"No, not really," she answered, "although their finale is supposed to be spectacular."

"Not nearly as spectacular as the finale we could create for ourselves," he said softly. "Everytime our mouths touch, I see stars. Don't you?"

"No," she said firmly.

"Liar," he returned. "I bet you think about making love all the time. I do." His voice darkened. "Only for you, Meg, would I show this much patience."

She didn't answer. She didn't want to pursue the conversation. But Clay apparently did. He took one hand off the wheel and rested it on her leg. The car was moving

83

slowly now, and the wind gently fanned her face. As far as Meg could tell, they were the only ones on the road for miles.

"Just imagine what it will be like," Clay said in a slow, suggestive voice, "when I undress you, when you first feel my hands on your bare skin. Think of the sensations it will arouse when my fingers brush your—"

"Stop it, Clay," Meg burst out. His words, the images conjured up, were doing strange things to her breathing. That now-familiar ache of desire was beginning to grow deep inside her.

He gave her a sideways glance. "Don't you like to think of me touching you? At night I lie awake thinking about running my hands down that beautiful body of yours. I imagine what it would be like to love you, to possess you." His voice grew husky. "Then I think how it would be to feel your fingers on my chest and my stomach."

Meg couldn't help herself. She slowly turned her head toward him, and her eyes traveled down to the dark hair showing beneath his partially unbuttoned shirt. Suddenly she was swept by an almost irresistible impulse to run her fingers through that hair, to feel him shudder as she touched him in ways she never had before. Shocked by her longings, Meg quickly turned her head and stared unseeingly at the passing countryside. But she didn't turn her head quickly enough. Clay looked over at her and read what was in her eyes. Abruptly, he pulled the car onto the shoulder of the road and brought it to a stop.

"What are you doing?" Meg demanded, trying to keep the panic out of her voice. She was alarmed by Clay's sudden movement but was even more alarmed by her own body.

Clay threw the car into park, turned off the engine, and slid across the seat to where Meg was sitting. Gently, he caressed her hair. As his hand slid from the top of her head to the bare skin of her neck, Meg leaned her head back against the headrest and stared into his eyes.

Between them, desire suddenly flared. They stared into each other's eyes as though mesmerized until Clay moved his hand from her neck to her mouth. Slowly he traced the soft curves of her lips, his eyes following the movement hungrily. Under the pressure of his finger, Meg felt her mouth part slightly. Clay gently let his finger move a little past her lips, touching her sensitive inner lips as he did so.

Meg gasped and pulled back. She hadn't realized how intimate a caress like that could be. Her heart was going wild.

"I think we should be going," she mumbled hoarsely.

"In a minute," he told her. He put his hands on both sides of her face. "I want you, Meg. God knows how much. Tell me you want me, too."

Meg looked up at him and knew it was useless to hide from the truth any longer.

"I do want you, Clay," she whispered, "but—"

Silver seemed to shoot out of his eyes. "No buts tonight, Meg," he murmured as his mouth took possession of hers.

Meg tried to hold herself back, but she couldn't. Her arms went eagerly around his neck. They kissed until time disappeared. Clay touched her hair lightly at first, then a moment later his hand ran down her shoulders to the soft swell of her breasts. Through the fabric of her shirt, the heat from his hand scorched her.

Meg could feel the hunger in his rigid body, and she knew what it cost him to release her and move back to the driver's seat. It wasn't much easier for her to let him go.

"I'm too old for this," he said ruefully as his eyes wandered over her face. Meg noted that his voice shook a little and his breath was coming unevenly.

"I haven't made love in a car since I was a teen-ager,"

he told her. "And even then it wasn't very comfortable." Before he started the car, he flicked her cheek with his finger. Meg smiled back at him a little tremulously. "You do strange things to me, woman. Every time I touch you, I go a little crazy."

Meg laughed a little uncertainly. "I know exactly what you mean."

Clay swung the car back onto the road and, after a moment of driving, patted the seat next to him.

"Come on over here," he said with that crooked grin that she was beginning to love.

Without a word she slid over and snuggled up to him. They sat in silence the rest of the way home.

Clay drove up the circular drive and stopped in front of the house. Gently, as though she were very fragile and very special, he helped her out of the car and walked her up to the front door. Meg had never felt so treasured, so cherished.

"I've got to put the car away," he told her as he opened her door, "but after that, I'd be happy to accept an invitation to come to your room. Or you can come to mine, if you'd rather."

"No, Clay," Meg said a little regretfully. "Not tonight."

"Not tonight," he repeated. He looked at her solemnly. "Not tonight, but soon. Is that what you're saying?"

"Perhaps," she murmured, not realizing how provocative she sounded. "It's been a long day," she told him. She was trying to inject a note of cool practicality into their conversation. "I'm hot and tired and—"

"I'm hot, too," Clay murmured.

"—and I want to take a shower and go to sleep," she finished firmly.

"I'll help you take a shower," Clay offered suggestively. "Just say the word and I'll wash you all over— your shoulders, your thighs, your—"

He reached for her, but Meg stepped away. She was

afraid that if his lips touched hers, if their passion for each other were allowed to ignite one more time, she *would* invite him up to her room.

"Goodnight, Clay," she tossed over her shoulder as she went inside.

"Goodnight, honey," he replied.

His voice echoed all the regret she felt, and it was all she could do to keep from turning back and throwing herself in his arms.

So much for guarding her heart, Meg sighed as she climbed the stairs to her room. She obviously had a lot of thinking to do. Clay had made what he wanted very clear. Now she had to decide what she wanted.

Inside her room, though, Meg found she didn't want to try to sort through her feelings. She didn't want to be practical and analytical, and she definitely didn't want to take a shower and go to bed. After a few moments of wandering restlessly from the dressing table to the bed to the comfortable overstuffed chair by the window, she thought of the swimming pool. She went over to her door, opened it, and listened for a moment. The house was dark and quiet. Clay had obviously gone to bed.

Quickly, Meg pulled on her bathing suit. It was a glorious night, and a relaxing swim in the moonlight would help her sleep.

Clay need never know, she told herself as she tiptoed through the silent house. His bedroom was nowhere near the pool, so she wouldn't disturb him.

When she reached the pool, she dropped her towel onto a chair and eased herself into the water, enjoying the cool, silky feeling on her warm skin. She swam vigorously to the far end, then lazily floated back. When she reached the pool's edge, she looked up. Clay, his legs slightly astride, was standing above her.

Meg's eyes traveled slowly upward, taking in his long, lean legs and the narrow waist that broadened to strong wide shoulders—an athlete's body. In bathing trunks,

Meg thought, there was only one word for Clay: Magnificent! Her eyes moved up to his face, and she discovered that he was smiling tenderly down at her.

"We seem to have had the same idea," he said as he lowered himself into the water.

Instinctively, Meg took a step backward and the tenderness in his smile changed to amusement.

"I thought I'd come down here and cool off," he told her. "But that was before I realized you were here."

Meg blushed. "I'll race you to the other end," she called.

Clay beat her easily as she knew he would, but the race banished the constraint she had been feeling. As soon as she touched the wall, he sprayed her with water. They splashed back and forth until Clay dove headfirst toward her. Meg turned and tried to swim away, but Clay was too fast for her. His hands circled her waist and, though she tried to twist away, he turned her effortlessly in the water and brought her up against his chest. Meg put her hands on top of his shoulders to steady herself, and Clay immediately let his hands slide down to her hips.

"I've wanted to feel your body next to mine all night long," he told her. His hands pressed her hips into his. "Feel how much I want you," he said.

She knew without him saying anything. Her eyes widened, and her legs tangled with his in the water.

"How do you feel, knowing you have such power over me?" he asked. His voice was serious and his eyes probed hers intently.

She shook her head slightly. "You're a sensual man," she told him trying to keep her voice light. "Any woman in a wet bathing suit could—" Her voice trailed off.

"Arouse me? Excite me?" He finished her sentence for her. "Perhaps. But not to the fever pitch you do. You make me feel like I'm on fire. No other woman has ever done that."

Desire was beginning to work its way through Meg's

body, and she realized that she was now clinging to Clay rather than trying to push him away.

"Have you ever made love in a swimming pool?" he murmured, his fingers caressing her through her swim-suit.

"No." Her voice was nothing but a whisper.

"Would you like to give it a try?" He bent over her and let his lips nibble at hers teasingly. "I promise not to let you drown."

"It's a little late for that," Meg said without thinking.

He gave her a knowing smile, and for a moment Meg wondered if he would try to make love to her in the pool. Panic registered in her eyes, clearly visible in the moon-light. When he saw it, Clay sighed.

"Are you ready to get out?" he asked instead.

"That sounds like a good idea," Meg told him. Her body was beginning to tremble a little—and not from the cold.

Instead of releasing her, he carried her up the pool steps and deposited her onto a cushion-covered chaise longue.

"I'll get a towel and dry you off," he said.

"I can dry myself," Meg protested as he walked to the other end of the pool for her towel.

"I'm sure you can," he answered. There was a wicked twinkle in his eyes. "But that wouldn't be nearly as en-joyable for either of us."

When he returned with the towel, she started to reach for it. He quickly stopped her.

"Don't move," he told her. "I want to look at you."

Meg leaned back and watched him as his eyes slid down her body, taking in the way her white swimsuit clung to her. His eyes ran over her like a caress. She wanted to look away as he devoured her, but she couldn't. A shiver worked its way down her spine.

"Has anyone ever told you that you have a beautiful

body?" he asked finally. He dropped down beside her and began to slowly pat her with the towel.

She shook her head. "Not recently," she said. She could feel the heat of his hand through the towel, and she was doing her best to ignore it.

Clay's attempts to pat her dry with the towel were turning into slow, lingering caresses.

"Well, take it from me," he said a little hoarsely. "You've got a beautiful body. And I'm willing to bet it's even more beautiful when all your clothes are off."

He raised his eyes to her face, and they stared at one another for a very long moment. Meg ran her tongue over her hot lips.

"Meg," Clay breathed. "My sweet Meg." He leaned toward her, and Meg met him halfway. Their lips joined and clung together for an endless amount of time.

"You've cast a spell over me," Meg murmured unsteadily when he finally drew away. She sank back against the chair. "I don't know how much longer I can resist you."

"Don't try," he whispered seductively. His face lowered over hers. Their lips were only inches apart. She could feel the warmth of his breath on her face. She stared at his mouth, anticipating what it would feel when it again touched hers. "Would you like me to kiss you again?"

Meg felt her heart skip a beat. "Yes," she whispered, her voice no more than a sigh. "Please."

Clay's mouth possessed hers more roughly this time. There was still tenderness in his touch, but she could also feel a new, demanding insistence.

"It's magic," he murmured finally. "Every time we touch, it's magic."

"I never imagined it could be so good," she confessed. Her fingers trailed slowly through the curling tendrils of hair covering his chest.

"And it gets better," he told her in a voice that

90

sounded a little fevered. His hand went to the back of her neck and with a deft, sure movement, he untied the two thin straps that held up her suit. Meg made a protesting movement, which he stilled with another kiss.

"Don't stop me," he muttered thickly. "It's all right. I won't rush you. We'll just go one step at a time."

At the look in his glittering eyes, Meg's protest died in her throat. She lay back in the chair and stared at him.

Slowly and confidently, he drew down the top of her swimsuit. Meg wanted to put up her hands to shield herself from his eyes, but her body was weak with desire, and she knew she wouldn't stop him. As he slowly eased the suit down to her waist, she could feel the late night breeze on her overheated skin. She could feel the wild beating of her heart, and she could feel Clay's silvery eyes trace her exposed breasts.

His hand brushed across her rib cage, and the ache inside her grew.

"Skin like silk," he muttered just before he bent his head.

When his mouth touched her breast, his lips caused such overwhelming sensations that Meg cried out. "We've got to stop," she managed to say somehow.

"Do you want me to?" he asked. He brushed her neck teasingly with his lips.

"No," she whispered. "No."

Clay immediately moved his mouth up to hers, and Meg arched toward him. She felt the harsh curling hair of his chest press against the softness of her own; then they seemed to melt into each other. Meg wanted their kisses to go on forever. When he captured her bare breasts with his strong warm hands, Meg heard herself moan somewhere in the back of her throat. Clay had turned her drunk with pleasure.

"Look," he commanded her.

She followed his eyes downward and saw the darkness of his hand against the paleness of her skin. Clay brushed his fingers across her tense nipple, and it seemed to grow even more tense. Meg looked at him helplessly. His eyes shone with passion as he watched, and she could see the effect it was costing him to exert so much control. Instinctively she covered his hand and her breast with her own hand.

"Don't be embarrassed," Clay said softly. "It's beautiful. I enjoy seeing the effect I have on your body."

"It's not that I'm ashamed or embarrassed," she said. "It's just that I've always thought of myself as a cool, reserved person. But when you touch me—"

"I know," he said. "The same things happen to me. All you have to do is lay one hand on me, and I go wild with desire. We have a power over each other. What's wrong with that?"

Meg raised troubled eyes to his. "I don't want you to be able to stir up feelings like this in me," she cried out. "Every time you do, you show me just how vulnerable I am."

"You're looking back again," Clay told her. "Don't look back. Trust me."

Meg shook her head, and tears filled her eyes. "I can't help it," she whispered miserably. "I want to trust you, but I'm afraid."

Clay's understanding surprised her. "I know," he said gently. "But you're learning to trust me. It won't be long before you realize that I don't want to hurt you. I just want us to share something very special."

Reluctantly, he pulled her suit up and retied the straps behind her neck.

"And now," he said wryly, "I think we'd better go in while I can still let you go."

Meg got unsteadily to her feet. "Thank you for being so understanding," she said. Her voice was as shaky as her legs.

"I'm trying," he said wryly. Then his voice grew rough. "But, Meg, I'm not usually a patient man. Don't make me wait much longer."

CHAPTER SIX

"I've got to fly over to Austin for a meeting this morning," Clay said to Meg a few days later as she was scrambling eggs and cooking sausage for breakfast. "Why don't you come with me?"

"Just like that?" Meg asked skeptically.

Clay could tell she was tempted. "Just like that," he replied. "We can spend the afternoon at my condominium on Lake Travis, then fly back sometime this evening."

"It sounds like a wonderful idea," Meg said a little reluctantly. All of eastern Texas was in the midst of a record-breaking heat wave, and a day spent at the lake sounded heavenly to her. "But who will fix lunch and dinner for the men?"

He shrugged. "They can forage for themselves," he told her. "They managed before you got here, so I suppose they can manage while you have a day off."

"Well, I do have some casseroles in the freezer that they can have for dinner," Meg said. She looked at the clock. "And I can put together a cold salad for lunch. That won't take long."

"You know," he said, "the men don't really like cold

salads." Clay grinned at her. He knew he had won. "They think salads are sissy food. They can have the casseroles for lunch, then grill some steaks and cook a few potatoes for dinner. That'll satisfy them."

"But that's such heavy food for weather like this," Meg protested.

He shrugged again. "They're tough. They'll manage."

Meg shook her head. "Heaven spare me from macho males. At least you like my salads."

There was a sudden twinkle in his eyes. "I don't dislike your salads," he conceded with another grin, "but, to tell you the truth, I'd rather have a steak, too."

Meg watched him for a moment. "I don't know why you bothered to bring me out here to cook for your men," she said. "It seems to me that everyone, including you, would be just as happy eating big hunks of cholesterol-laden meat for every meal with a few eggs thrown in at breakfast."

Before Meg could move away, Clay crossed the room and took her in his arms. The twinkle in his eyes was even more noticeable up close. "You know very well why I brought you out here," he said, planting a kiss on the tip of her nose, "and cooking had nothing to do with it."

"As far as I'm concerned, cooking had everything to do with it," she replied primly. She stepped out of his arms and went back over to the stove.

"Are you sure?" he asked teasingly. His eyes were warm and caressing. "Every now and then, I've seen a little thaw in that cool manner of yours."

"That's just your imagination," she told him.

"Well, you certainly take your work seriously," he admitted grudgingly. "Every time I see you, you're busy."

"I just want to make sure you get your money's worth," she said. As she talked, she arranged some dishes on the counter so the men could serve themselves.

At her words, something glinted in his silvery eyes,

and he began to move toward her again. "In that case—" he started in a low voice.

Meg didn't let him finish; she knew better than that. She hurried to the back door, where she rang the bell signaling that breakfast was ready. Then she made her way over to the door leading out of the kitchen.

"I'll be ready in thirty minutes," she threw over her shoulder as she left the kitchen.

"Just you wait," he said to her softly. His words were part promise, part threat.

An hour later, she and Clay lifted off from Broken Rock's private airstrip. Meg leaned back and watched Clay's hands at the controls of the twin-engine Cessna. He was a relaxed, confident pilot, and Meg, who normally didn't like to fly, felt perfectly safe with him.

It was a smooth, uneventful ride, and when they reached Austin, he gave her the key to his condominium and put her in a taxi.

"I'll be there as soon as I finish my meeting," he promised as the taxi driver pulled out. She looked back and waved good-bye. As she watched him growing smaller and smaller, she was a little surprised by her sudden feeling of loneliness. Clay was moving into her heart, whether she wanted him to or not.

When Meg reached his condominium, she found it was something straight out of a magazine. Everything about it was delightfully luxurious. The living room was done in a white-on-white theme, including walls, couches and rugs, and the kitchen was a cook's dream, complete with every appliance a woman could want. She peeked into each of the three bedrooms and found they were as perfect as the rest of the apartment, done exquisitely in a pale color scheme.

It's gorgeous, Meg thought in awe, but it's hardly a place for children. She could just imagine what children, wet and dirty from the lake, would do to the white carpet and the linen-upholstered furniture.

She wondered why that thought should suddenly pop into her head, and why she should find it so disgruntling.

She changed into her bikini, went out for a quick swim, and, by the time Clay arrived, she was sunning herself on the wide balcony overlooking the lake. Though it was as hot in Austin as it was at Broken Rock, just knowing the lake was there made the heat more bearable. Clay, however, didn't seem to think so.

"You look miserable," she said sympathetically to him as he dumped a bag of groceries onto the kitchen cabinet. She pulled on her bathing suit cover-up and tied it firmly.

"And you look wonderful," he replied. "If I look miserable, it's because I am. Whoever invented suits for men was a sadist. It must be over a hundred out there," he went on. "Days like this make me grateful for air conditioning."

"Put your trunks on," Meg suggested, "and we'll go for a swim."

"I'm not sure I want to go back out there," he said, "not even for a swim." His eyes swept hungrily down her body. "Why don't we stay inside and open the bottle of wine I bought? I have an idea things could get interesting." His eyes moved back up her body, pausing boldly at the curve of her breasts showing beneath her cover-up.

"A swim will do you good," Meg said firmly. With an effort, she ignored the tingling his look was producing throughout her body. "I'll put these things away while you're changing."

"I'd rather have you help me in the bedroom," he murmured suggestively. "I'm so hot, I'm not sure I can get out of these clothes by myself."

Meg trembled a little at the image his voice conjured up, but her voice remained steady. "What did you buy?" she asked as she began lifting little white carry-out boxes from the bag.

"Lunch," he answered. "There isn't anything to eat here. Hadn't you noticed?" He watched her for a moment, then peeled off his suit coat and began unbuttoning his shirt.

"As a matter of fact, I hadn't," Meg told him, keeping her eyes firmly fixed on the groceries she was taking out of the bag. "Everything in the kitchen is so perfect, I was almost afraid to open the cabinets or the refrigerator. I wouldn't want to leave fingerprints anywhere."

"Don't you like my apartment?" he asked abruptly. For some reason, Meg knew her answer really mattered to him.

"I love it," she told him. "Who wouldn't? But you have to admit, it doesn't look very lived-in."

"We'll change that," he said quickly. "We'll come here as often as you like."

They looked at each other across the large kitchen, communicating wordlessly. When Clay left to change into his trunks, she shook her head. He was making it very difficult for her to remember that she didn't dare trust him with her heart.

"Sit down," Clay told her an hour later. They had just come in from swimming at the lake, and they were both ravenous. Meg looked at him in surprise.

"I'm going to serve you lunch," he said. "You wait on me at the ranch, so it's my turn to wait on you here."

"It's my job to wait on you at the ranch," she reminded him.

"That may be," he said, "but you take better care of me than any cook I've ever had before. Now sit down."

Meg obeyed. Clay could be very masterful when he wanted to be. "I didn't know you could fix anything besides eggs," she said.

"I didn't say I was going to cook anything," he told her. "I said I was going to serve you lunch. Didn't you look in any of those little white carry-out containers you put in the refrigerator?"

"Not a one," she replied cheerfully. She watched him for a moment as he began lining things up on the counter. Then she got to her feet.

"Curiosity certainly won't kill this particular cat," he observed. His voice changed as she started to leave the room. "Where are you going?"

"I'm going to put on some clothes. I can't eat lunch in my bathing suit."

"I don't see why not," he countered swiftly. "I'm going to."

Meg looked a little flustered. She didn't want to sit across from him wearing nothing but her bikini. She knew she'd feel uncomfortable. Just the way he looked at her made her uncomfortable. Clay read her thoughts easily.

"I can't promise not to stare," he told her, "because I enjoy looking at you."

Meg felt herself blush slightly. She reached for her wrap and began to put it on.

"Don't," Clay commanded softly. "Don't hide yourself from me. You've got a beautiful body," he said in a low, intimate voice.

Meg shivered a little at the look in his eyes.

"Of course," he told her with a searching glance that went straight to her heart, "it's pure hell for me to be able to look and not touch, but it's a torture I'll undergo willingly."

Meg knew just how he felt. Ever since he had put on his trunks, she had been experiencing an almost irresistible urge to run her hands across his bronzed chest. The very thought of it made her fingers tingle.

"Just relax," Clay said, "and I'll bring you a glass of wine."

Meg sat down at the glass-topped table, and in an instant Clay had put a placemat and silverware in front of

98

her and filled her wineglass with a cold, clear white wine. A moment later, he brought her lunch. She looked at it in surprise. It was nothing less than a work of art.

"Cold pasta salad," he said imperturbably, "surrounded by an assortment of marinated vegetables." He added a little more wine to her glass with a flourish.

"It's gorgeous," Meg said as she gazed at the tiny whole zucchini and carrots, the julienned green beans and the tiny florets of cauliflower and broccoli intermingled with the pasta. Across the top of the salad was a cluster of whole shitoki mushrooms, neatly tied in a bow with a scallion stalk. She shook her head in amazement. "I thought you didn't like salads."

"You wouldn't expect me to have a woman up to my apartment with seduction in mind and then serve her roast beef sandwiches, would you?" he asked in mock horror. "This is supposed to be a very romantic meal."

"It's a delicious meal, anyway," she said as she dug in. She decided she'd be wise to ignore the first part of his sentence, although she knew, of course, exactly why he had brought her to the lake. "How are you going to top this at dinner?"

"I'm ordering dinner from a French restaurant a few blocks away," he told her with a smile. "Arranging this on the plates just about exhausted my culinary skills."

Meg couldn't help laughing. She was sure Clay wasn't as helpless as he made himself sound.

"Actually," Clay said as they ate, "I had an ulterior motive in mind when I brought you out here."

Meg dropped her eyes to her plate. She knew all about Clay's ulterior motives. Clay noted the heightened color in her face and grinned.

"I like the way your mind is working," he said a little wickedly, "but that can hardly be said to be an ulterior motive. I've been pretty open about my desire to make love to you."

Meg looked up, and for a long, tension-crackling moment his eyes held hers. In them she could see his hunger for her, and it made her ache. Then she managed to return her focus to her plate.

"I'm going to ask you to do me a favor," Clay said.

Much to Meg's surprise, he suddenly sounded a little hesitant. What could this favor be? she wondered with some consternation. Normally Clay wasn't reluctant to ask for anything he wanted.

"I will if I can," she replied a little doubtfully.

He smiled with obvious amusement. "You're very cautious all of a sudden," he observed. "I'm not that cautious. I can't think of anything I wouldn't do for you if you asked me to."

Including giving up your freedom? Meg thought cynically to herself. She was both dismayed and surprised at herself to silently admit that a part of her, anyway, was hoping for a future with Clay.

"Would you like me to swim the English Channel?" Clay asked. "I'd even walk over hot coals if you wanted me to."

Meg smiled a little wearily. He obviously didn't expect her to take him too seriously. "What is this favor?" she asked.

"I'd like to have some business acquaintances out to Broken Rock for dinner in a week or so. Do you think you could plan something for me?"

Relief washed over her. She hadn't known what to expect, but it certainly wasn't this. This would be child's play to her. "Of course I can. In fact, I'd enjoy doing it. How many people do you expect to invite?"

"Two dozen," he hazarded, "give or take a few."

"Do you want it to be formal or informal?"

"Formal," he said firmly. "People are always more impressed by a formal dinner party, and I'm going to invite a few politicians who need to be reminded, in a friendly sort of way, of how impressive I can be."

Meg gave him a thoughtful look. She'd read a lot about

100

Clay Beaumont the sophisticated man-about-town, and she knew a lot about Clay Beaumont the rancher. But she didn't know much about Clay Beaumont the business- man. It would be interesting to see him in operation.

"I don't want you to do any of the actual work your- self," Clay told her. "You can hire people to do that. I just want you to plan it and serve as my hostess, if you will."

That hesitant note was back in his voice. It gave Meg the idea that he wasn't as sure of her as he claimed to be.

"I'd love to be your hostess," she said gently, "but, of course, I'll prepare the meal for you."

"I'll be the envy of Houston if you do," he told her. "I'll have my secretary get out the invitations tomorrow, and you can take it from there." He got to his feet. His eyes were warm on her face. "Now we can either curl up on my bed for a nap or go out for another swim. I vote for the nap."

"I vote for the swim," Meg said instantly. "But first I think we should wash the dishes."

"The dishes!" Clay exclaimed. "This isn't very roman- tic," he complained as he picked up his plate and fol- lowed her into the kitchen. "Next time we'll use paper plates."

When they finished, Clay tossed the dish towel onto the table. "I think we deserve a reward." He opened the refrigerator and pulled out an icy bottle of champagne.

"This means we'll have more dishes to wash," Meg said mischievously as he rummaged in the cupboard for two champagne flutes.

"Oh, no," Clay said firmly. "I've done all the dishes I'm going to do for one day. We'll throw these in the fireplace."

He opened the champagne with an expert twist of the wrist, then poured the clear bubbling liquid into the tall glasses and led her into the living room. "Can you think of a more perfect place for us to make love?" he asked.

His voice was husky, and at the sound of it Meg felt something catch in her throat.

"Is that why you brought me here?" she asked a little uncertainly.

"I brought you here so we could be alone," he told her seriously. "At the ranch it's almost impossible to get you by yourself. One of the men is always around. And you don't seem to do anything to discourage them," he finished up accusingly.

"They're protection," Meg murmured provocatively. She took a sip of champagne. The bubbles tickled all the way down her throat.

"I'm well aware of that," he told her a little angrily. "But here you don't have any protection. It's just you and me and the magic we create between us."

Meg lifted her glass to her lips and gulped at the champagne. With deft hands Clay reached over and took it from her. He put it on the table beside him.

"I don't want you to drink too much of that," he said with a meaningful smile. "I want you to know, to feel what happens between us."

Meg ran her tongue over suddenly dry lips. It's going to happen, she thought to herself. It's going to happen, and there is no way I can stop it. I don't even *want* to stop it.

"We're adults, Meg," Clay murmured. His eyes dropped to her lips. "We're adults who are capable of giving each other a great deal of pleasure." He raised his hand and gently traced her lips with his finger. "I want to please you," he muttered hoarsely.

"And I want to please you," she whispered back.

He moved closer to her on the sofa. "You do please me. Everything about you pleases me. You're all I've ever wanted in a woman." His hand left her lips and encircled the back of her neck. "Don't ask me to stop this time, Meg. I need you too much to stop."

Meg stared back at him helplessly. His desire had kindled her own, and she was beginning to ache all over.

"Kiss me," she breathed. Her voice was so soft that Clay barely heard it. He didn't, however, miss the invitation in her eyes.

"I'm going to," he muttered. "I'm going to kiss you in places you've never even thought about."

He leaned forward. Slowly, tantalizingly, his lips moved toward hers. Meg watched them with feverish impatience. By the time their lips met, she was on fire. Eagerly her arms slid around his neck, and she pulled him close. They clung together for a long, hot moment, then Clay loosened her arms slightly and leaned her back against the soft, wide sofa.

"Let's take it slowly," he murmured. "I've waited too long for this to rush. Besides, we've got all afternoon and all night."

Clay stretched out beside her, propped himself up on his elbow, and looked down at her. As his eyes devoured her, Meg found she was a little nervous.

"Shouldn't you close the curtains?" she asked faintly.

"Why? No one can see in. Anyway, I like the light. I want to be able to see you. Don't you want to see me?"

"I'm not sure," she answered. Her voice was even more faint.

Clay grinned at her knowingly. "Just relax," he murmured. "Just relax and let it happen. I'll take care of everything." Provocatively, his leg tangled with hers, and he shifted his weight so that it was partially resting on her.

Meg reached up and traced his face with her hand. As soon as Clay felt her touch, he leaned forward and began kissing her neck. Slowly his lips worked their way downward, until Meg was shivering with pleasure.

Very slowly and very gently, he slid his hand under the straps of her bathing suit and untied the top.

Meg felt she should protest—common sense told her

she should protest—but she didn't. The time for protest was past, and she knew it.

"You are very beautiful," Clay murmured thickly as he gazed at her creamy white skin. "More beautiful in daylight than moonlight, if that's possible."

His silver eyes blazed down at her, and under the intensity of his gaze Meg could almost feel her breasts growing fuller and heavier.

His hand stroked them tenderly. "You're so soft," he muttered as his eyes continued to devour her.

"Clay," she whispered.

He looked up and saw the confusion in her face. "Don't worry," he told her. "I won't rush you. We'll go at your speed, not mine."

Then he lowered his head and began kissing her with such tenderness that it made Meg want to cry. Finally, he drew back a little.

"Do you see how good it is between us?" he asked.

"It's wonderful," Meg murmured. Her eyes met his, and again she felt that jolt of electricity. "Don't stop," she whispered.

Clay made a sound that was a low moan. His lips went to her breasts this time, and expertly his tongue aroused her, turning her pink softness into firm peaks.

Meg heard a sound come from the back of her throat. She felt herself arch against him. Her heart was pounding furiously, and she felt as though she could no longer breathe. Clay had become everything she wanted, everything she needed.

Clay rolled over onto her, and as his weight pressed her into the softness of the sofa, she could feel how much he wanted her. She wiggled beneath him and a groan escaped him.

"Don't do that, you little temptress," he told her. "You'll push me over the edge, and I'm not ready for that yet."

Meg smiled up at him seductively, letting Clay know

how much she wanted him. Slowly she ran her hands over his strong, muscular back. She could feel his heart pounding against hers, and it gave her a heady feeling.

"Meg," he said urgently. His eyes burned into hers. "In another moment, I'm not going to be able to stop."

Her smile grew even more Delilah-wise. "I don't want you to stop," she breathed.

Clay's eyes flashed, and he muttered something under his breath. Then he began kissing her with such force that everything disappeared for Meg; everything but the sensations he was so expertly producing. His lovemaking grew slower and wilder until Meg could stand it no longer.

"Clay," she whispered.

"I know," he answered. Unsteadily he got to his feet and lifted her into his arms. "We'll finish this in the bedroom."

He had taken two steps when the doorbell rang. The sound of it shattered the silence. Clay stopped in the middle of the room.

"Ignore it," he told Meg firmly.

She closed her eyes and pressed her face against Clay's chest, but it did no good. The doorbell rang again and again.

Clay swore out loud. His face was thunderous. "The person on the other side of that door must have a death wish," he muttered. Reluctantly, he put Meg down.

"I'm sorry," she told him helplessly. She reached for her bathing suit cover-up.

He brushed her face with his thumb. She could see the frustration in his eyes. "I'm sorry, too. I'll get rid of whoever that is, then—"

The bell rang again. Clay strode to the door with long angry strides and yanked it open.

"Clay, old buddy!" exclaimed the man on the other side. He stepped past Clay and walked uninvited into the living room. "I heard you were here. Are you staying long?"

"Just for the day," Clay said tightly. "Meg, this is Buck Henderson."

"Hi," Meg said. She looked at Buck with relief. "That name sounds familiar."

Although Clay was obviously furious, she was suddenly glad they had been interrupted. Clay was very adept at weaving spells around her, and she was glad to have had this one broken. She had come close, too close, to giving in to him, and in the morning she was sure she would have regretted it.

Now, she thought to herself a little ruefully, she had to find a way to keep him from picking up where they had left off. That wasn't going to be easy.

Buck grinned at her. "I play a little football," he admitted.

"Why aren't you at practice or something?" Clay demanded. Meg had put on her bathing suit cover-up, and he knew that this particular moment had passed. It didn't make him any more cordial.

"Training camp doesn't start till next week," Buck told him easily.

"Would you like something to drink?" Meg asked before she remembered there was nothing but champagne.

"No, thanks. I just stopped by to invite you two to a barbecue I'm having down by the lake."

"That sounds wonderful," Meg said, jumping at his insinuation. At the barbecue, surrounded by people, there would be no opportunity for Clay to renew his assault on her defenses. And there would be no opportunity for her to crumble at his touch, either.

"Good!" Buck said. "Just come on down whenever you're ready."

Much to Meg's amazement, Buck seemed completely unaware of the tension in the room, even though it was thick enough to cut with a knife. As for Clay, he was far from being the gracious host. All he could do was glower.

"Close the door behind you when you go, Buck," he said coldly.

"Sure thing," Buck said obligingly. He wasn't the least bit put out by Clay's behavior. "See you later."

"You did that on purpose," Clay said accusingly when they were alone again. His voice was cold and hard.

"Did what?" Meg asked, playing for time.

"Accepted his invitation. You deliberately told him we'd go to his barbecue so you wouldn't have to be alone with me." Clay folded his arms over his chest and stared down at her.

Meg took a deep breath. "Try to understand. It's just that everything's moving so quickly."

"Quickly, hell!" Clay burst out. "You want me as much as I want you. But every time we get close to each other, you throw up obstacles."

"I didn't throw up any obstacles this time," she pointed out. "I wasn't going to stop you."

His anger eased a little. "I know," he said. "That's why I don't understand why you accepted that invitation."

"I don't want to be hurt," Meg told him quietly.

"And I don't want to hurt you," Clay answered. He stared at her in frustration. "Why won't you believe that?"

"I do believe it," she answered. "But you might not be able to help yourself."

"And just what does that mean?" he asked angrily.

That means I'm falling in love with you all over again, Meg thought to herself. And I don't want to go back to Houston with a broken heart.

"You've been so patient with me," Meg said. "Just be patient a little longer."

His anger disappeared. "I'll wait for you for the rest of my life if I have to," he said.

107

Meg stared at him. How she wished he meant that.

"But don't expect me to like it."

She smiled at him a little tremulously. "Why don't we go on down to the barbecue?" she suggested.

"We might as well," he grumbled. "It's obvious that my attempts at seduction have failed. So why not salvage what's left of the day."

Meg's smile was more natural this time. Clay had a terrible temper, but fortunately he didn't stay angry long. He held out his hand, and after a moment Meg put hers in it. Together they went down to the lake.

When they got there, Buck gave them each a big smile and a can of beer.

"What have you got to eat?" Clay asked.

"Texas barbecue, ribs, the usual stuff," Buck answered.

"Good," Clay told him. "I'm starved."

Meg looked at him in astonishment. "We just had lunch. How can you be hungry?"

"All we had for lunch was salad," Clay reminded her. "Besides, it's nearly six o'clock."

"Is it?" Meg asked in surprise. "I had no idea it was so late."

Clay grinned, and something in his grin made her face grow warm. "Time flies when you're having fun," he laughed.

Meg resolutely looked away and began asking Buck about his team's chances for the coming year. While they were talking, Clay went to the buffet and returned a few minutes later with two plates filled with food.

"How can you eat all that?" Meg asked as she took the plate he offered and began to nibble. Clay was devouring the food on his plate.

"I have to," he replied. "Afternoons that end like this one drain my strength."

"Oh, they do, do they?" Meg said. "Do many of your afternoons end like ours did?"

He grinned at her, and Meg felt her heart flip over. Everything was suddenly a little brighter.

You've really got it bad, she told herself, if one little smile does all that.

"Fortunately not," he answered. "In fact, this afternoon was a first for me." He winked at her. "It's a good thing, too. Many more would be very bad for my ego."

Meg gave him an even look. "Your ego will survive," she said dryly. She was surprised at how jealous she suddenly felt. How many women had he entertained in that sumptuous apartment of his? she wondered.

Clay read her mind easily. "I've never brought another woman here. I wanted this to be our place. We'll come again soon, very soon."

"I hope we can," Meg answered softly.

"And next time I'll see to it that nobody bothers us— even if it means hanging a do-not-disturb sign on the door."

"That would be a little bit obvious," Meg protested.

He shrugged. "It looks like that's the only way I'm going to be alone with you." He reached over and wiped some barbecue sauce from her chin. "I don't know about you," he said in a more provocative tone, "but eating with my fingers like this always brings out the primitive male in me. If you'd like to go back up to my apartment, I'll show you what I mean."

Their eyes met for a brief moment, then Meg looked away. She could imagine all too vividly what he meant.

"No thanks," she said breathlessly. "I think I'd rather stay here and enjoy the barbecue."

"Coward," he said imperturbably. "One of these days you won't be so anxious to avoid me."

"I'm not anxious to avoid you now," she told him a little shyly. "I just think it's—wise."

"I've never had much use for conventional wisdom," he told her. His eyes were suddenly bitter. "I did the wise thing once, and I've regretted it ever since."

Meg looked at him in surprise. She wanted to question him, but something in his face warned her off.

"I'm sorry," she said softly. She reached over and put her hand on his arm. At her touch, the tightness in his face eased slightly.

"It's in the past," he said, "and I'm not concerned about the past. I'm only concerned about the present and the future."

Do we have a future? Meg wanted to ask. She didn't, though, because she was afraid of the answer.

Dusk was settling in, making everything seem a little softer, a little more romantic, and music began to play.

"Would you like to dance?" Clay asked.

Other couples were beginning to dance along the lakefront. Meg smiled up at him. "I'd love to."

With the grace of a panther, he got to his feet and swung her into his arms. Meg slid her arms around his neck and pressed herself against him. Clay groaned slightly.

"What's wrong?" Meg asked. She pulled away so she could see his face.

Clay's arms tightened around her until they were again chest to chest, thigh to thigh. "Nothing's wrong," he murmured, "except for the fact that we aren't alone and I can't do the things to you that I'd like to."

Meg's knees trembled for a moment. "That's exactly why we aren't alone," she told him lightly.

"I'm well aware of that," he growled. "Do you have any idea what it does to me to hold you like this and not be able to make love to you properly?" His hands moved slowly up and down her back.

Meg peeked up at him. "Denial builds character," she said primly. Her eyes, though, were teasing.

"I don't want to build character," Clay said emphatically. "I've got all the character I can use. I want you."

"This is all you're going to get of me tonight," she said. "So you might as well enjoy it."

110

"Oh, I am enjoying it, in a perverse sort of way. I want all of you, but if I can't have that, I'll take what I can get. The least you could do is take off this damned terry cloth thing you're wearing over your bathing suit so I can touch you."

Meg just laughed. She had no intention of taking anything off. Instead, she rested her head against his chest and closed her eyes. Listening to the sturdy thud of his heart gave her a warm feeling.

"Much as I hate to break this up," Clay said finally, "I think we'd better go."

"So soon?" Meg asked dreamily.

Clay bent his head, and his lips found hers. It was a heart-stopping kiss, just as he had meant it to be.

"Let's stay here for the night," he murmured. "We can fly back to the ranch early tomorrow morning."

Meg turned her head so that he couldn't see how tempted she was.

"Stay with me," he urged her. His voice was low and persuasive. It sent little chills up and down her spine. "I'll make love to you all night long."

She felt her heart begin to beat more frantically. She wanted to stay with him; she was beginning to want it more than anything.

He could sense her weakening. "Remember how it was between us this afternoon. It will be like that again, only better." His hand found the bare spot at the back of her neck, and he began caressing it with a stroke that was almost hypnotic.

"The men—" she murmured.

"To hell with the men," he snapped jealously. "Sometimes I think my men mean more to you than I do." He cupped her face in his hand and gently brushed her cheek with his thumb. "You're an enchantress, Meg," he whispered. "You do things to me I wouldn't have thought possible."

Meg stared up at him. "You're pretty adept at weaving

111

spells yourself," she murmured unsteadily. "All you have to do is touch me and . . ." her voice trailed off.

"I know," he told her. "Let's stay here tonight, Meg," he urged her again. "Let's stay here and fill the night with our own kind of magic."

It took a great deal of willpower, but Meg managed to tear her eyes from his. The urgency in them had almost compelled her to say yes.

Instead, she shook her head slowly. "I'm just not ready," she told him.

"But this afternoon—" he began in agonized tones.

"I know," she interrupted. "This afternoon I wouldn't have stopped you. But tonight I feel differently."

"I don't understand," he told her.

"I don't understand it myself," Meg confessed. She raised troubled eyes to his face. "Please don't be angry, Clay. I just have to be sure."

He dropped a kiss on her forehead. "I'm not angry, honey," he said gently. "Just disappointed and a little frustrated. But I told you we'd go at your pace, and I meant it. When we make love, I want you to give yourself wholeheartedly. Anything less wouldn't be fair to either of us. Now, let's go find Buck and say good-bye."

An hour or so later, they flew back to the ranch. They didn't talk much as they traveled through the dark, starry night, but the silence was warm and companionable.

When they landed at Broken Rock, Clay had only one thing to say.

"You won't escape me so easily next time," he told her.

Meg didn't answer. How could she tell him she no longer wanted to escape?

CHAPTER SEVEN

Meg stood on the expansive flagstone terrace behind Clay's house and looked around her with satisfaction. Everything from the table decorations to the food was ready for Clay's dinner party. All she needed now were the guests.

Mother Nature had cooperated beautifully, she thought gratefully. The heat wave had broken earlier in the week, leaving cooler, drier air in its place.

The rosebushes surrounding the terrace were blooming profusely. Not only were the pink and white flowers pretty to look at, but their scent lingered in the air. Stationed around the edges of the terrace like sentries were big terra cotta pots filled with a profusion of lush, cascading flowers.

Three round tables, each seating eight, had been set for dinner. Meg had covered them with long, graceful lace cloths that picked up the pink in the rosebushes. The tables were set with an elegant array of crystal and silver, and at each place setting there was a single pink rose in a small crystal vase. Clay had said he wanted an impressive dinner party, and Meg had pulled out all the stops. Her carefully created menu was composed of showy but easy-to-fix dishes, most of which she had prepared ahead.

All in all, the planning of the evening had been fairly effortless. She hadn't needed any help with the food, but she had hired three black-coated waiters to serve the dinner and two women for last-minute kitchen preparations.

What she would wear had concerned her far more than the food or the table settings. Clay had never seen her in anything more dressy than a denim skirt, and she suddenly wanted to look glamorous, sophisticated, and alluring. She had taken a day off and gone into Houston, where she spent far too much money on a gown made of white gossamer silk. The gown looked Grecian from the front with its graceful lines, but the back plunged dramatically down to her waist, leaving a creamy expanse of skin visible. When Meg tried on the dress, she had known at once that she had to have it. The skirt had a tantalizing swirl to it when she moved, and the silk felt whisper-soft against her skin. Entranced by the dress, she had splurged on a tiny wisp of lace and silk to wear under the gown. It wasn't her idea of underwear at all, but it allowed the gown to fall in an unbroken line to her feet.

Now she stood on the terrace knowing she looked better than she ever had before. Her wispy brown hair framed her face beautifully, and her big blue eyes glowed with excitement.

A wolf whistle behind her brought a faint flush of color to her face. She turned to find Clay standing in the terrace door staring at her. The look on his face told her what he thought. It even justified the outrageous amount of money she had spent on the outfit she was wearing. With long strides, he crossed the terrace.

"I've never seen you look so ravishing," he said softly as he took her hand and raised it to his mouth. Meg felt her skin tingle pleasurably as his lips brushed it. He was making her feel very feminine and very desirable.

She couldn't help staring back at him. Clay always

looked wonderful both in the jeans he wore around the ranch and in the exquisitely tailored suits he wore to his office. He had the kind of body that looked good in anything. But in evening clothes he was more than wonderful —he was magnificent.

"You look pretty ravishing yourself," she answered. He was still holding her hand, and she made no effort to free it. Instead, she looked at him, noting the way his white dinner jacket accented the breadth of his shoulders and the black pants emphasized his long, powerful legs.

"That's a good word choice," he told her. "I feel ravishing—I feel like ravishing you. Why don't we call off this damned dinner party and spend the evening alone together? We haven't been alone since that day at Lake Travis."

"Stop fantasizing and tell me what you think of the way the terrace looks."

"It's wonderful," he said impatiently.

Meg didn't know whether to laugh or cry. She was sure he hadn't even looked around him.

"Meg," he began. His voice sounded strangely tortured. "Since we've been back from Lake Travis, I've kept my distance. I've tried to let things between us develop at a more natural pace. I've tried not to make you feel rushed."

"I know you have," she said gently, "and I appreciate it. I know it hasn't been easy on you."

"Easy!" he said explosively. "That's an understatement. It's been pure hell."

"Would it make it any easier for you if I told you it's been hard on me, too?" She raised expressive eyes to his, and for a long moment Clay stared down at her.

"Meg," he murmured finally. He pulled her into his arms and held her gently to him. "My sweet Meg. Are you finally starting to believe in me a little?"

Strangely enough, during the last ten days or so since they had returned from Austin, she had begun to believe

115

that Clay was interested in something more than a brief affair. He had been so thoughtful and so considerate that Meg was beginning to dream of a future for both of them. There had been no words of love, no hint of any kind of permanence, but she had begun to feel that it was her turn to do a little giving, her turn to show Clay that she trusted him.

Now she gave him a sexy smile, then watched the shock in his face as the message registered. It was the same smile she had given him that afternoon at the lake, the smile that meant surrender.

"Damn these people," he said violently.

At the same moment the doorbell rang. The party had begun.

Clay managed to pull himself together and greet his guests. Meg could see, though, that he wished they were anywhere but at Broken Rock. She was beginning to feel the same way herself. Every time she looked at him, something blossomed in her heart. She was in love, and there was no point in hiding from that fact any longer.

She didn't have much time for thinking, though. She was kept busy making sure everyone had drinks, and several times she had to step into the kitchen to check up on the hired help.

"When are we going to eat?" Clay demanded impatiently. He had followed her into the house and caught up with her just as she reached the kitchen door. Meg turned in surprise. She hadn't realized he was behind her.

"In about fifteen minutes," she told him. "If you're hungry, have some canapés."

"I'm not hungry," he told her a little angrily. "Food is the last thing on my mind, and you know it. I just want to feed these people so they'll go home and leave us alone. We need to talk," he said urgently. "Meg, I saw something in your eyes earlier that—"

"Later," she said firmly. One of the uniformed maids

116

she had hired for the evening came through the kitchen door and gave them a curious glance.

"You're enjoying this," he said accusingly. "I'm in agony, and you're enjoying it."

"How can you say such a thing!" she exclaimed.

"I can't concentrate," he swept on heedlessly. "I can't think of anything but you. How can I go out there and make small talk? I ache with wanting you, but with all these people around, I can't even touch you."

The maid stepped around them on her way back to the kitchen. Clay glared at her, and she scurried through the door like a frightened rabbit. The look on his face was enough to frighten anyone.

Meg put her hand on his arm. "After everyone leaves, we'll talk," she said soothingly.

"We'll do more than talk," he muttered under his breath.

"But until then—" She broke off as the maid again hurried out of the kitchen. This time there was a stack of plates in her hands. She cast an apprehensive look at Clay, then kept her eyes firmly fixed on the floor.

"What in the name of heaven is that woman doing?" he asked testily.

"She's setting up the dessert buffet," Meg answered. "I thought we'd have dessert and coffee in the living room."

"Thank God for that anyway," he said fervently. "I don't know how long I'll be able to sit down at one of those tables with you next to me knowing I have to keep my hands to myself. Who's idea was this dinner party, anyway?"

"I won't be sitting next to you," she told him a little nervously. He was beginning to alarm her a little. She had never seen him like this before.

"Where will you be sitting?" he asked ominously. His face was thunderous.

"At one of the other tables," she told him gently. "I thought it would be better if we split up."

He gave her an incredulous look. "Change the seating arrangements!" he ordered in a voice that allowed for no argument.

"Please, Clay," she said a little desperately. He looked as though he were going to erupt. "I've worked hard to pull this evening together, and I did it all for you. Don't ruin it."

She was relieved to see him look a little sheepish. "I'm not behaving well at all, am I?" he asked ruefully. He touched her cheek. "I'm sorry, honey," he told her. "I just want to be close to you."

"I know," she said. "But this isn't the time."

"You're right. It's just that I've waited so long for those barriers you've built around yourself to come down. Earlier, before my guests arrived, I thought I saw you lowering them, and I guess it drove everything else from my mind." He smiled down at her, a smile guaranteed to turn her bones to water. "I'm sorry."

"It's all right," she said softly. When he smiled at her like that, she'd forgive practically anything. "Now I've got to check on things in the kitchen, or we'll never have any dinner."

"Go ahead," Clay told her. "I'll try to be patient." He turned and headed toward the terrace. "Just tell them to hurry it up in there," he tossed over his shoulder as he walked away.

How Meg got through the dinner, she never knew. Clay stared at her constantly; his eyes seemed to devour her across the heads of his guests. She was sure everyone could read the expression on his face.

Aside from that, the dinner was a big success. Her food received raves, and Clay's guests seemed genuinely to be enjoying themselves.

Meg's own nervousness increased as the dinner wore on. The way Clay kept staring at her was almost embarrassing. She had no idea how Clay was going to react

118

once his guests left, and she found that a little frightening. She wasn't at all sure she'd be able to manage him.

When the long dinner finally ended, people began drifting into the living room for dessert and coffee. Meg had also set up a small bar there to serve brandy and liqueurs. She herself was finally able to relax. Clay seemed to have disappeared for the moment. He was probably having a discussion with one of his guests, she thought, grateful to whoever was keeping Clay away for a few minutes. But her peace didn't last long.

"I think you're needed in the kitchen, Meg," Clay interrupted as she was talking to a couple of his guests. "A small crisis seems to have developed."

Meg excused herself and hurried off toward the kitchen. Clay followed at her heels.

"This way," he said as she reached the hall.

She looked at him in surprise. "The kitchen's not that way."

"Did I say the kitchen?" he asked blandly. "I meant the library."

"What are you up to, Clay?" she asked suspiciously.

He took her arm and pulled her toward the library. "What makes you think I'm up to anything?" His face was the picture of innocence.

"For one thing, I know you. For another, what kind of crisis could possibly be developing in the library? It certainly wouldn't be anything that required my presence."

"That's where you're wrong," he said blandly. "Your presence is just what's needed."

By this time, they were in the library. No one else was there, and the lights were dim. Clay firmly closed the door behind them.

"I'm the crisis," he told her. Some of the tension had left his body, and there was a mischievous twinkle in his eyes. It was obvious he had something in mind. "If I don't get some time alone with you—"

"What about your guests?" Meg asked. She was a little

119

nonplussed by his behavior. "We can't just hide in the library for the rest of the evening."

"Who said we're going to hide in the library?" he asked. "Anybody could walk in here and find us. No, that wouldn't do at all, and I have someplace a little more private in mind."

Before she could ask him any more questions, he swung her up effortlessly into his arms and crossed the room to the french doors, which led outside. A moment later, he was lightly running toward the barn, and Meg was clinging tightly to his neck.

"What are you doing?" she wailed. "Where are we going? Someone will see us."

"No one will see us," he assured her. "It's too dark for that. Besides, they're all on the other side of the house."

"We can't leave your guests!" Meg tried to convince him. "They'll miss us."

"They won't even know we're gone," he returned calmly.

"You're mad," Meg told him as he kicked the barn door closed behind them. Part of her was exasperated, but part of her couldn't help being flattered by the lengths he had gone simply to be alone with her. "You've lost your mind." Nothing else could account for his behavior.

"You're damned right I have," he replied. "I've lost my mind over you, and now it's time to do something about it."

With the door closed, it was so dark in the barn that Meg could barely see, but Clay made his way unerringly to the ladder that led up to the hayloft. With one hand he held Meg to him; with the other he began to climb the ladder.

"We'll fall!" she cried. "Put me down!" Her arms tightened around his neck.

"We won't fall," he said confidently. "Anyway, I can't

120

put you down. You couldn't possibly get up the ladder in that dress and those ridiculous high heels."

"I don't want to go up the ladder," she protested. She closed her eyes and buried her face in his chest. With each step up, she half-expected the two of them to go crashing to the floor.

"Of course you do. You just don't realize it yet."

When they reached the top of the ladder, Clay carefully put Meg on her feet. Then he pulled the ladder up behind him and stowed it neatly next to the wall. She watched in silence as he took a folded blanket from the top of a bale of hay and spread it over some of the loose hay that filled the loft. Next, he pushed open a small trapdoor in the roof above them, flooding the loft with silvery moonlight.

"Sit down," Clay invited, giving her a gentle push.

Meg sat.

"Where did this blanket come from?" she asked a little breathlessly. It hadn't taken her more than a minute to realize that she was marooned up here with Clay. She couldn't get down without the ladder, and she couldn't possibly move the ladder by herself. She would have to stay in the loft until Clay was ready to leave, and judging by the expression on his face, that wouldn't be for some time yet.

"I put the blanket here myself a few minutes ago," he told her.

So that's where he was, she thought. And she'd been so sure he was having a private discussion with one of his guests. "Do you go around all of eastern Texas stashing blankets here and there just in case you find yourself in the area with a willing female?" she asked tartly.

"Are you willing?" he returned a little wickedly. "I certainly hope so."

"That's not what I meant, and you know it," she told him.

121

"I don't know anything of the sort," he replied smoothly.

Meg just looked at him. She could see him very clearly in the moonlight, and it seemed to her that he was looking very pleased with himself.

"We really should get back," Meg tried once more.

"Later," Clay said.

"But this is crazy," she burst out a little nervously.

"Crazy or not, we're not going anywhere." He knelt in front of her and took one of her feet in his hands. "Right now I want you to relax and be comfortable." Gently he slid her shoe from her foot and began massaging her instep. "You've been running around all night in these silly high-heeled things. Don't your feet hurt?"

"A little," she admitted. His hands on her foot were doing strange things to her pulse.

"Why do you wear them?" He moved to her other foot and began massaging it.

"Vanity, I suppose," Meg answered lightly. It was getting harder and harder for her to speak normally.

"You don't need shoes like this to make your legs beautiful," he said. He dangled her slippers from his finger by their flimsy heel straps for a moment, then casually tossed them aside. "You'd look good in sneakers."

With one fluid movement, Clay was beside her, and she was suddenly lying in his arms. She realized at once that she was where she wanted to be.

"I've wanted to do this all night long," he murmured. "Every time I looked at you, I wanted to feel you lying next to me, I wanted to kiss you and make love to you."

He propped himself up on one elbow and gazed down at her. His other arm stretched possessively across her stomach. Meg gazed back at him. She no longer wanted to leave the loft.

"Woman," he said only half-teasingly, "I don't think you have any idea of what you do to me."

122

She reached up and ran her fingers over his lips. At her touch, his eyes narrowed slightly.

"Maybe not," she said softly, "but I know what you do to me."

"Oh?" he murmured seductively. "And what's that?"

"One look from you, and my bones crumble," she whispered. "When you touch me, you make me forget that anyone or anything else exists."

His eyes glinted suddenly in the moonlight. "That's what you do to me," he told her unsteadily. "I've never felt anything like this for a woman before. Oh, Meg, I'm going crazy with wanting you."

Instead of answering, Meg lifted her head and pressed her lips to his. Clay responded by gathering her to him with a force that drove the breath from her body. A moment later, he laid her back on the blanket.

"Does this mean what I think it means?" he asked huskily. "Are you finally going to give us a chance?"

"I'm going to do my best," she answered.

His eyes darkened perceptibly. "You won't regret it," he promised her. "Not now, not ever."

He bent down and took possession of her mouth. It was a long kiss, filled with passion and an aching tenderness that left Meg feeling almost drugged.

"How often do you bring sweet young things up here to seduce them?" she asked shakily.

"You are a sweet young thing," he replied. His own voice was none too steady. "You even taste sweet. In fact, you taste so sweet that I can't get enough of you."

He bent toward her until this time her arms went around his neck and she pulled him down to her. She was kissing him with all the pent-up hunger she'd been hiding.

"That's right," he whispered encouragingly. "Kiss me back. Kiss me like you mean it."

For Meg, time disappeared. Clay became the center of her universe. Slowly and patiently he coaxed her body to respond to his. After a few moments his fingers slipped under the straps of her gown, and he carefully slid the dress down over one arm, then the other. Meg shivered, and a tremor worked its way down her spine. When his lips touched her breast, she felt her heart go wild.

"Do you want to stop?" Clay asked in a hoarse voice. His breath was coming rapidly. "If you do, it will have to be now or never."

Meg looked at him through passion-clouded eyes. "No," she whispered, "I don't want to stop."

His eyes glittered wildly. He ran his hand over her soft skin; then his lips claimed hers again. It was a demanding kiss, and Meg felt herself yielding to it, to him. She could feel the hunger in him, and she could feel her own hunger growing to match it.

Possessively, he slid his hands under her body and lifted her to him. He was just sliding her dress down to her hips when a sound shattered the stillness, splintering into a thousand pieces the magic Clay had drawn around them. Someone was opening the door to the barn.

Meg sat up and gave him a dazed look. He gathered her to him protectively and cradled her in his arms. She could hear the pounding of his heart, and she could feel her own as it beat against her rib cage. It seemed to her that the loft was filled with the sound of their heartbeats. Surely the person standing below could hear them, too.

Meg looked up at him anxiously. He gave her a reassuring smile and put his finger over his lips. He shook his head very slightly.

"Clay," a female voice called from below them. "Are you in here?"

Meg stiffened. They *had* been missed.

"Of course he's not in here," a second voice said a little irritably. "It's completely dark in here. What would he be doing in a dark barn? For that matter, what would anyone be doing in a dark barn?"

"Well, he's not anywhere else," the first woman said defensively, "and Senator Price is looking for him."

Meg shifted in Clay's arms. Senator Price, she was thinking. Common sense was returning to her, and with it came a feeling of guilt. She and Clay should be in the house looking after their guests. What had come over her? she wondered a little wildly.

Clay seemed to sense her thoughts. He put his hand over her mouth and held her so tightly that she couldn't move.

"What was that?" the first woman said sharply. Meg could hear her take a step forward.

"What was what?"

"I thought I heard something. Shh. Listen."

"I don't hear anything," the second woman said impatiently. "You probably heard a cat or a mouse. Let's get out of here."

"All right," the first woman said reluctantly. "I suppose you're right. I never knew a barn could be so spooky," she added as they left.

They closed the door behind them, and as it shut Meg struggled out of Clay's arms.

"We've got to go back," she said urgently. "People are starting to miss us." She began to pull her dress up over her shoulders.

Clay stopped her with a lazy gesture. "We were interrupted at the lake—and that was more than enough for me. We're not going to be interrupted again."

"Your guests—" Meg started.

"They can wait," he said huskily. "I can't." He gently pushed Meg back on the blanket. "I've waited too long for this. I'm not waiting any longer."

"But—"

Clay silenced her with a kiss. As his lips touched hers, Meg felt the world beginning to drift away from her again. She knew she should protest, she knew she should

125

insist that they leave, but Clay's nearness was draining her willpower.

"You don't really want to leave, do you?" Clay whispered into her ear. His breath tickled.

"No." She sighed, turning her head so that their lips met again. "No, I don't."

"Meg, my darling," he murmured a moment later, "you taste like starlight and roses." Carefully, he slid her dress down past her hips, then pulled it from her body. With a casual flick of the wrist, he tossed it onto a bale of hay.

Meg thought she would faint as his eyes traveled hungrily down her body. They seemed to be shooting sparks as they devoured her. "Perfection," he whispered. His fingers traced a leisurely path down her body that left Meg trembling. "There's only one flaw that I can see."

"What's that?" she managed to ask.

His eyes moved to the wisp of silk that served as her underwear.

"This," he said. He slipped his finger under the tiny thread of elastic that held the panties up, and Meg felt her heart go wild. Slowly and provocatively, he tugged them slowly down over her hips, and a moment later they went sailing through the air to join her dress.

"Now you're perfect," Clay muttered under his breath. "Every curve is perfect." He sat back on his heels and stared intently at her.

Meg laughed softly. It was a soft, seductive laugh, a stranger's laugh. She'd never heard herself sound like that. The look on Clay's face was heating her blood. It was making her feel sensual and desired in a way she'd never even dreamed of. She stretched languorously, and in response something dangerous flickered in Clay's eyes.

"I want to touch you," she told him, still using that seductive voice that belonged to someone else.

"All in good time," he replied hoarsely.

He stood up and shed his jacket with lazy grace. His

126

tie and shirt quickly followed. His movements seemed to say that he had all the time in the world, but Meg could see the rapid rise and fall of his chest. She knew he was almost out of control.

The rest of his clothes joined the pile on the bale of hay, and he stood towering over her. It was her turn to stare at him, and she did. Never had she seen anything so magnificent.

"Don't look at me like that," Clay groaned. "I can't stand it."

He dropped down beside her and gathered her to him with such poignant tenderness that Meg felt more than desired. She felt cherished, even loved. Clay hadn't said he loved her, but love was with them in the loft. She could sense it.

"I've dreamed about this moment," he told her in a voice that made her ache. "I've dreamed about how it would feel to make love to you; how it would be to feel all of your beautiful body under my hands."

"I hope I won't disappoint you," she whispered a little shyly. She began to run her hands over his chest and shoulders, marveling as she did so at his physical strength.

"You could never disappoint me," he told her.

He stretched out beside her and began coaxing her to follow him to new heights. Meg followed willingly, abandoning herself to the touch and feel of him against her body. His hands slid slowly over her, stopping at her hips so that he could lift her slightly.

"Don't be afraid!" he whispered.

Meg fought her way back from the exquisite pleasure Clay was creating long enough to open her eyes. He was poised over her, and his brow was covered with sweat. She knew he couldn't hold back much longer.

"I'm not afraid," she told him. Her eyes were loving. "How could I be afraid when I'm with you?"

"I won't hurt you," he swore softly as his hand moved below her waist. "I'll never hurt you."

"I know," she murmured. As Clay watched, her eyes widened for a moment, then closed again.

"This is what it's like when two people care for each other," he told her huskily.

"It's wonderful," she murmured. "It's wonderful, and you're wonderful."

"You're the wonderful one," he murmured, although he was almost beyond talking. "I've wanted you so much —I've waited so long"—there was suddenly triumph in his voice—"and now you're mine."

He pressed himself against her, and she felt herself being swept up and up to new heights and glorious fulfillment.

"Skyrockets," she whispered a few moments later when her breathing finally allowed her to speak.

"Hmm?" Clay muttered interrogatively.

"Skyrockets," she repeated dreamily. Her body felt sated and languorous. She never wanted to move again. She wanted to stay in the loft with Clay for the rest of her life. "I thought I saw skyrockets."

Clay propped his head upon his hand and looked down at her. "You're wonderful, Meg," he told her. There was a hint of rich, warm laughter in his voice.

Meg reached up and traced his features with a finger. "You're wonderful yourself," she said softly.

"I'm glad you think so. Next time it will be even better."

"Is that possible?" Meg asked with a smile.

He grinned. "You know what they say. Practice makes perfect, and I intend to see to it that we get lots of practice."

"That's fine with me," she murmured provocatively.

As Clay stared down at her, his grin faded and his eyes flashed. When he spoke, his voice was urgent. "You're mine now, Meg. You belong to me. I have no intention of sharing you with anyone else. Don't forget that."

"I won't forget," she promised with her heart in her eyes. It was a promise she knew she'd never forget.

Feeling utterly content, she pulled him down to her. He rested his head on her breast until their heartbeats returned to normal.

"The party," she said finally.

"Damn the party," Clay replied succinctly.

Meg sat up and brushed her hair away from her face. "I think we should be getting back," she said regretfully. "If we don't, people will be forming search parties."

"I suppose you're right," Clay grumbled. He sat up reluctantly. "I just don't want this moment to end." He cupped her chin with his hand and raised her head so that she was looking into his eyes. "When this party is over and all the people have gone home, will you come to my bed?"

In the moonlight, Meg blushed. Clay saw the telltale color and chuckled softly. "If it weren't for these people waiting for us, I'd make love to you again here and now," he said.

"So soon?" she asked a little confusedly.

"You've gotten into my blood. Will you come?" he asked again.

She nodded shyly, and he planted a quick, triumphant kiss on her lips. Then he got to his feet and began sorting out their clothes. Meg reached for her dress, but Clay kept it from her.

"I took the dress off," he said, "so I should be the one to put it back on you."

While she watched, he dressed himself with lightning speed. Then he slid her panties up to her hips. Meg felt something stir deep inside her as he slowly smoothed the fabric over her stomach. He continued the caress until Meg started to feel weak. She looked up at Clay and

129

found he was staring at her with a mischievous look on his face.

"So soon?" he asked wickedly, mimicking her voice.

She felt the color flood her face, but Clay merely laughed.

"Desire has nothing to do with a clock," he told her. "It has to do with people. I think I could make love to you without stopping for the next three days and still not have enough of you."

"I didn't know it could be so wonderful," Meg told him softly.

"And it's going to be even better," he promised.

"You keep saying that, but I don't see how," Meg murmured.

"I'll just have to show you." Clay dropped her dress over her head, then helped her to her feet. "We'd better hurry and get back down to the party while I still can." His hands lingered around her waist, and he stared into her eyes until Meg pulled away.

"The ladder," she reminded him a little breathlessly. If they didn't leave now, she had the feeling they wouldn't leave at all.

He let go of her with obvious reluctance and dropped the ladder over the side of the hayloft.

"Back to the real world," he said regretfully as he helped Meg to the floor of the barn. At the bottom of the ladder, he knelt and slid the high-heeled sandals back onto her feet.

Hand in hand, they walked over to the french doors outside the library and slipped back inside. Meg blinked a little as her eyes adjusted to the brightness. The room, which had been dark when they left, was now ablaze with light.

"How do I look?" she asked. She was suddenly a little nervous about going back into the living room. She was sure everyone would take one look at them and know exactly where they had been and what they had been doing.

"You look like a woman who's been loved to within an inch of her life," Clay said with a slow grin.

Meg tried not to blush. That was exactly how she felt. "That's not what I mean," she said hastily. "I mean, how is my makeup and my hair?"

"If you want an objective opinion," he told her seriously, "I'm the wrong person to ask. As far as I'm concerned, everything about you is breathtakingly beautiful."

Meg gave him a heartfelt glance. She raised herself up on tiptoe and pressed her lips against his.

"I think I'll go upstairs for a few minutes," she said. "I want to make sure there's no hay clinging to my dress."

"I'll come with you," he offered instantly.

She couldn't help laughing. "You will not. You'll pay some attention to your guests. I'm afraid they've been neglected shamefully," she added ruefully.

Clay put his hands on her shoulders. "Are you sorry we neglected them?" he asked softly.

"No," Meg told him with a mischievous smile. "I'm not."

"Good," he said, dropping a kiss on her nose. "Neither am I. Now run along and do whatever it is you want to do upstairs."

Meg hurried up to her room, combed her hair, and renewed her makeup. Before she went back downstairs, she checked in the mirror for bits of straw. Fortunately, her dress was practically crushproof. It hadn't suffered much for being tossed onto a bale of hay.

After a quick peek into the kitchen to make sure everything was all right, she rejoined Clay's guests. Much to her relief, the party was going well. Apparently they hadn't been missed by anyone other than Senator Price and the two women who had come looking for Clay.

As she entered the living room, Clay's eyes met hers

over the heads of the crowd. He immediately hurried to her side.

"Being loved agrees with you," he murmured softly. His eyes swept her face.

Meg looked around her quickly. She hoped no one was close enough to hear him.

"There's a glow to you that I've never noticed before," he went on thoughtfully. "You look radiant."

"I feel radiant," she confessed. "If there is a glow, it's all because of you." Her eyes met his, and he grinned happily.

"Honey," he drawled, "I can't tell you how good you are for my ego." Then his smile faded. "Senator Price wants to meet with me after everyone leaves," he told her gently. "I wouldn't have agreed, but it's important. I don't know what time I'll get to bed, so you'd better not wait up."

"I see." Meg's heart fell. She had been looking forward to being close to Clay.

He stood directly in front of her so that she had to look up at him. "We'll have other nights," he promised. "Lots of them."

Meg smiled back a little tremulously. "I know," she said. "It's just that I'm—"

"Disappointed?" he filled in. "So am I. More disappointed than you can imagine. But—"

"Business comes first," Meg said with a little ache in her heart. All her fears were suddenly back. He had gotten what he wanted. Now she was just another in a long line of conquests.

Clay's voice sharpened. "No," he said, "business does not come first. Not usually. It's just that this is something I've been working on for quite a while, and it seems to be coming together now. Believe me, Meg," he added softly, "I wouldn't have had this happen for the world. I wanted tonight to be our special night." He looked at her helplessly.

Meg's smile was a little stronger this time. "It has been special," she murmured. There was laughter in her voice. "I'll never forget it."

Clay gazed down at her. "Neither will I."

CHAPTER EIGHT

In the morning Meg came down to breakfast with dark circles under her eyes. She had stayed awake most of the night tossing and turning and worrying about Clay. She loved him, but did he love her? Last night, he had said everything but those three little words. Unfortunately, they were words that mattered desperately to Meg. Common sense told her that she had to be more careful now than ever before. Rosy dreams of a future together were nice, but she had to be prepared for the heartbreak that she was beginning to think was inevitable.

Feeling suddenly shy and a little wary, she started breakfast.

Clay came down to breakfast thirty minutes later wearing a tailored suit, a tie, and a troubled expression on his face. Something was wrong, very wrong.

"Senator Price has arranged for some meetings for me in Washington," he told her at once. "He wants me to testify before a Senate subcommittee. That's why he was trying to find me last night."

Meg's heart sank. She hadn't expected this. "When are you leaving?" she asked quietly. She kept her eyes on the

French toast she was preparing. She was almost afraid to look at him.

"Right away." He took her face in his hands and tilted her head back so that she had to look at him. "As far as I'm concerned, this couldn't be a worse time for me to leave. Believe me, Meg, I don't want to go. But I've got to."

Meg smiled in what she hoped was a reassuring manner. "It's all right."

"No, it's not all right," he exploded. "It's anything but all right. Unfortunately, there's nothing I can do about it."

She searched his face. She saw worry, uncertainty, and guilt in his eyes. Could he possibly be regretting what had happened between them? she wondered with a terrible sinking feeling. It seemed impossible to her. Last night had been so beautiful, so full of wonder. And yet . . . Shaken, she turned away.

Clay stared at the back of her head in frustration. "Come with me," he said suddenly.

Meg hesitated for a second, then shook her head. She was tempted, but considering what she had seen in his eyes a few minutes ago, it seemed safer to refuse. Perhaps they needed some time apart, time to think about where they were going.

"I'll be in meetings all day," he told her, "but we'd still have the evenings together."

Meg turned back to face him. "I think I'd rather stay here," she said. "Here I've got some work to do; in Washington I'd just be at loose ends."

"You could sightsee," he offered tentatively. He had a feeling she wouldn't like that, and he was right.

"Along with all the other tourists who flock to Washington in the summer?" she asked with a smile that was more natural this time. "No thanks. Uncle John and Aunt Helen took me to Washington one summer when I was in high school. I know what it's like."

Clay gave her a worried look. "I don't like the idea of leaving you," he said. "Not now. Last week, next week—anytime would be better than now." A little angrily, he jammed his hands into his pockets and regarded her balefully.

"Now seems like a very good time for you to leave," she told him carefully. "It will give us a chance to sort through our feelings."

"That's exactly what I don't want you to do," Clay said unexpectedly. He took a deep breath. "Can't you see I'm afraid that I'll come back from Washington and find you gone?"

Meg stared up at him in surprise. "That hadn't occurred to me," she said honestly.

"Not yet maybe, but it might if you spend a lot of time 'sorting through your feelings,' as you call it," he said in frustration. "I know how I feel. I've always known. Why don't you?"

I do, she wanted to say, but she didn't. She couldn't. Instead, she shook her head helplessly. The two of them seemed to be talking at cross purposes this morning, and there wasn't enough time to straighten things out.

Clay seemed to have the same feeling.

"Oh, Meg," he said with a strange note in his voice. "There are so many things to say, so many things for us to talk about, and now just isn't the time. I wish I didn't have to leave."

"So do I," she said softly.

There was a noise outside the kitchen door. One of the men was coming in for breakfast.

"Promise me you'll be here when I get back," Clay said urgently. "Promise me you won't run away."

"I'll be here," Meg promised softly. It was a promise she meant to keep. Her guard slipped for a moment, and she looked at him with her heart in her eyes. Clay took a step toward her.

The door opened, and the man walked in. Meg looked

136

away from Clay, and he stopped where he was. Clay glared at him, and the man looked around him as though wondering what he had done wrong.

"Morning, boss," the man said a little uncertainly.

"There's nothing good about it," Clay snapped back. He stared at Meg for a moment. She was breaking eggs into a bowl and didn't look at him. Clay suddenly turned on his heel and stormed out of the kitchen.

"What's biting him?" the cowhand asked curiously.

Meg blinked back the tears that had unexpectedly filled her eyes, and she forced herself to sound cheerful.

"He has to go to Washington this morning, and I don't think he wants to."

"Better him than me" was the cowboy's final comment.

Clay was gone nearly a week, and they were the longest six days of Meg's life. She wanted him back at the ranch desperately. She wanted to know that the evening they had together before he left had been the beginning of something, not the end. He called her several times, and she should have found the calls reassuring, but she didn't. For one thing, he sounded preoccupied and irritated when he called. His meetings weren't going well and, though she didn't realize it, he was frustrated by the delays that were keeping him from her. For another, he said nothing personal during their conversations.

Then one afternoon she walked in from some shopping to find Clay slumped back in a chair at the kitchen table.

"Hi, honey," he said feebly.

Meg dumped her groceries onto the counter and knelt down beside him. Something in the way he was sitting frightened her.

"What's wrong? Are you sick?" she asked gently. She put her hand on his forehead as she spoke. He was burning up, and he was as white as a sheet.

"No," he replied shakily. "I'm never sick."

Meg got to her feet. "I'm calling the doctor."

As she hurried over to the telephone, Clay stared at her. "No doctor," he said firmly. "I just need some rest and some good food. It's all that hot air and humidity in Washington," he added a little incoherently. With that he tried to get up, but he collapsed onto the floor.

Meg stared at him in horror, then rushed to the door and called two of his men to carry him up to bed. While they took him up to his room, she put in a frantic call to the doctor. Fortunately he was in, and he promised to come right over to Broken Rock.

She was sponging Clay's overheated body, trying desperately to bring down the fever, when Dr. Brandt arrived. The men had taken off all of Clay's clothes before they had covered him with blankets. Meg would have been embarrassed if she hadn't been so worried.

With a frown on his face, Dr. Brandt examined Clay. Finally he stood back and shook his head.

"He's got a bad case of the flu," Dr. Brandt said. "He'll have to stay in bed for at least a week."

"That's ridiculous," Clay muttered crossly from the bed. He had woken up and was looking at them with a stubborn glint in his eye. "I've got work to do."

Meg flew over to him and sat on the edge of his bed. "You're very sick," she told him. She took his hand and was shocked at how lifeless it felt. "You're going to need someone to take care of you."

"You take care of me," he told her.

"I don't know," she said uncertainly. "I'm not a nurse."

"You'll do fine," Dr. Brandt said heartily. "He doesn't really need a nurse. He just needs a lot of TLC."

Meg tried not to blush. "I suppose I could manage that," she said stiffly.

"It will be a lot of work for you," the doctor warned her. "I doubt if Clay will be an easy patient."

"I'll manage," Meg said a little grimly. The responsibility frightened her, but she knew she couldn't let Clay down.

"That's my girl," he muttered from the bed.

"I'll have some medicine sent out," the doctor said briskly, "and I'll write out some instructions for you. I've given him an injection that should hold him until the medicine gets here. I'll be back tomorrow morning. I want his fever down by then."

Meg nodded soberly. "I understand."

"I'll call your aunt before I leave here," Dr. Brandt went on. "I'm sure she'll want to come over and help."

Meg didn't protest. She knew she couldn't possibly give Clay the care he needed and cook for the men at the same time.

"Thank you," she said gratefully.

"See that you do as this young lady tells you," Dr. Brandt told Clay as he left. Then he turned to Meg for one last word of warning. "Get that fever down."

But instead of going down, Clay's fever continued to rise. By nighttime, he was delirious.

"Meg," he kept calling. "Meg."

"I'm here," she said over and over. It didn't seem to do any good. He kept calling her again and again.

"Don't leave me, Meg," he muttered as he tossed and turned feverishly. He couldn't seem to lie still for more than a few seconds.

Meg crooned soothing words to him as she would have to a child. Her hands shaking, she sponged his body with cool water and alcohol. She was frantic with worry. The medicine, the sponge baths, the damp towel across his forehead—nothing seemed to be doing any good. Clay continued to move restlessly in the bed, calling out deliriously for her every few minutes.

Finally, around four the next morning, just as she was about to phone for an ambulance, the fever broke and Clay fell into a deep untroubled sleep. Meg sat by his bed for the rest of the night watching him. She was completely exhausted, yet she was afraid to leave him for fear the fever would return.

Morning brought Aunt Helen, and Meg was never so glad to see anyone in her entire life.

"How is Clay this morning?" Helen asked worriedly. She had come directly up to Clay's bedroom, and the two of them were speaking in very low tones. "When I talked to Dr. Brandt yesterday, he told me Clay was very sick."

"He's better," Meg told her. "His fever broke a few hours ago, and he seems to be sleeping peacefully now."

"He's turned the corner, then," Helen said decisively. "The doctor will be here soon, and he'll be pleased."

"What time is it?" Meg asked a little dazedly.

"Nearly eight o'clock," her aunt told her.

"Eight o'clock!" Meg exclaimed with dismay. "I completely forgot about the men. I wonder if they've had anything to eat." She started to get up.

"Don't worry about the men. They can take care of themselves for another hour or so," Helen told her. She pushed Meg back into her chair. "What about you? When did you eat last?"

Meg thought for a moment. "I don't remember," she mumbled. "Sometime yesterday."

Helen moved toward the door. "I'll go down and make you some breakfast," she said firmly. "You've got to eat to keep up your strength if you're going to nurse Clay properly. I'll start some soup, too," she mused. "He won't be able to eat anything solid for a while."

"Aunt Helen?" Meg asked a little diffidently.

Helen regarded Meg from the doorway. She knew exactly what Meg was thinking. "I'll check on the men, too," she promised.

"Thanks," Meg said gratefully. "And thanks for coming to help. I don't know what I'd do without you."

Helen blew her a kiss and bustled down the stairs. A few moments later, she was back with a tray full of piping hot food. Meg hadn't moved an inch while she was gone.

She still was sitting in the same chair, and her eyes were still anxiously glued to Clay's face.

"Eat this while it's hot," Helen said as she moved a small table in front of Meg's chair.

"It's delicious," Meg said as she took a bite of the aromatic omelet her aunt had prepared. "I didn't realize how hungry I was."

"You've been too busy to think about food," her aunt said dryly. "When you're finished eating, I'll stay with Clay and you can get some sleep."

Meg shook her head. "I don't want to leave him until the doctor gets here. I can't help worrying," she said suddenly. "Look how deeply he's sleeping. Our talking doesn't bother him in the least. Is that normal?"

"I'd say it's entirely normal," Helen told her. "It's a good healing sleep. His body needs to repair itself." She looked at her niece thoughtfully. "All this is a bit beyond the call of duty, isn't it?" she asked lightly. "Surely Clay could have gone to the hospital."

Meg nodded. "I wanted him to," she confessed, "but Clay refused. What could I do? I had to take care of him. There wasn't anybody else to do it."

"Are you sure there isn't more to it than that?" her aunt asked innocently.

Meg gave her a sharp look. "I'm not sure I know what you mean." Her voice was stiff. "Clay's an old friend. Naturally I want to help him."

"Clay has always been fond of you," Helen said. She seemed to be picking her words very carefully. "There was a time when I thought you were fond of him. When you moved out here after all these years, I thought that you and he—" Her voice dwindled off.

Meg picked up her cup of coffee and stared into it. She didn't know what to say to her aunt. Everything between Clay and her was too uncertain for her to say much of anything.

"I moved out here for the reason I told you," she said

finally. "Clay needed a cook. He asked me to help him out, and I agreed."

"But you're in love with him, aren't you?" her aunt pressed gently.

Meg shot an apprehensive look at the bed. She didn't want Clay to hear any part of this conversation. Fortunately, he was still sound asleep.

"I don't know," she said. "And I certainly don't know how he feels about me."

"Do you remember that summer several years ago when you and Clay were dating?" Helen asked suddenly.

Meg tensed. Why was her aunt bringing that up now? "Yes," she said in a voice designed to discourage further conversation.

"I've always wondered if something would have come of that summer if your uncle and I hadn't interfered." Helen's voice was regretful, even sad. "We meant well, but—"

"I don't remember you and Uncle John interfering," Meg said. She gave her aunt a puzzled glance.

"We thought he was too old for you; too old and far too sophisticated," her aunt went on musingly. She stared at Clay, thinking that she might have had Meg nearby all these years if they had let them alone. Perhaps by now there would have been children for her to love.

"I know you did," Meg said wryly. "You told me that often enough, as I recall." She looked over at her aunt's face and her voice grew gentle. "And you were right. Clay was too old for me. He didn't love me, and I didn't love him. We were just having fun. Nothing would have come of that summer."

Her aunt still looked troubled. "I'm not so sure of that," she said unhappily. "You see, there's something—"

Meg held up her hand. Someone was coming up the stairs. "It's the doctor," she said, trying not to let her aunt see how glad she was to have their conversation interrupted.

Helen got up and began collecting Meg's dishes. "I'll take the tray downstairs," she said tactfully. "Good morning, Horace," she said as she passed Dr. Brandt in the hallway.

"Good morning Helen," he said. "Beaumont's a lucky fellow to have you and your niece looking after him. I hope he realizes it."

Helen smiled. "There's coffee in the kitchen, and I'll be happy to fix you some breakfast if you'd like."

"That sounds wonderful," Dr. Brandt answered fervently. "But I don't want to put you out."

Helen laughed again. "You won't be. Just come down to the kitchen whenever you're ready."

"Good morning, Meg," Dr. Brandt said as he entered the room. "How is the patient doing?" He looked toward the bed. "Much better, I see."

With his words, Meg's spirits rose. Clay's deep sleep didn't seem to alarm the doctor in the least. "His fever broke a few hours ago, and he's been like this ever since. Nothing seems to wake him up," she added a little doubtfully. "I wasn't sure if such a deep sleep was normal."

"It's the best thing in the world for him," Dr. Brandt said. He took out his stethoscope and listened to Clay's heart. "Good, good," he said. He continued his examination while Meg hovered anxiously. Finally he closed his black bag and stood up.

"He's much better," Dr. Brandt said. "He couldn't have gotten better care at the hospital."

"I'm glad to hear that," Meg said a little unsteadily. "There were times last night when I thought—"

The doctor looked at her sympathetically. "You did a good job." He looked back over at the bed. "He'll wake up after a while, and knowing Clay, he'll probably be hungry. Let him have some of your aunt's good, nourishing soup. Don't give him anything heavy or hard to digest." He chuckled. "I imagine he'll complain. When he does, you just tell him it's doctor's orders."

Meg smiled. She was sure Clay would complain.

The doctor picked up his bag. "I want you to get some rest, young lady," he told her sternly. "If you don't, your aunt will be nursing both of you, and she's not as young as she used to be."

"I'll get some rest," Meg promised.

"Good. I'll be back tomorrow." With a kindly smile, he disappeared down the hallway.

Meg sat back down on the edge of the bed. Sound asleep, Clay looked young and vulnerable. She leaned over and smoothed his hair from his face. Lightly, she dropped a kiss on his forehead. When she pulled back, she saw that his eyes were open, and her heart jumped.

"Good morning, sleepyhead," she said. "How do you feel?"

He grimaced. "Like I was run over by a cement truck," he croaked. "Can I have some water?"

Meg poured some water into a glass, then slid her arm under him to prop him up. Clay took a sip, then pushed the glass away.

"You make a good pillow," he whispered weakly. He closed his eyes and promptly fell back asleep.

Meg cautiously removed her arm. She started crying out of sheer relief. Clay was going to be all right! She hadn't realized until that moment just how much his illness had frightened her.

I've really got it bad this time, she told herself as she wiped the tears from her eyes. She moved from the bed to a nearby chair where she could watch him.

"The doctor says he's doing very well," Helen said when she returned half an hour later. If she saw the redness around Meg's eyes, she ignored it.

"Yes," Meg said gratefully, "and he woke up just long enough to say he felt like he had been hit by a cement truck."

"That sounds like Clay," Helen said appreciatively. "Now you go and get some sleep." She held up a hand to stem Meg's protest. "You'll wear yourself out if you don't get some rest. If it makes you feel any better, I promise I won't leave him until you get back."

Meg smiled at her aunt. "It makes me feel a lot better," she confessed. She gave Helen a quick kiss as she left the room.

Back in her own room, Meg took a quick shower and then tumbled into bed. She was asleep before her head hit the pillow.

Much to her surprise and everyone else's, Clay turned out to be a model patient. He complained about the food he was getting, of course, but as long as Meg stayed in his room with him, he seemed happy just to lie in bed.

"What's that?" he asked a couple of mornings later when she came into his room carrying a large bowl. A fluffy white towel was draped over her arm.

"Warm water," Meg told him, hoping he wouldn't notice her heightened color. "I'm going to give you a sponge bath." Dr. Brandt had suggested it, and though she wasn't looking forward to it, she had to admit that a bath would be a good idea.

Clay evidently thought so too. "That sounds like fun," he said wickedly. Meg took one look at the expression on his face and laughed in spite of herself. "You're incorrigible," she told him.

"I'm going to enjoy this," he commented as she unwrapped a fresh bar of soap. "I could use some excitement after three days in bed." His eyes glinted suddenly. "Are you going to wash all of me?" he asked in a soft voice.

"Certainly not," Meg said primly. She turned the sheet down to his waist. "This is a sponge bath, not a shower."

"A shower sounds like a good idea." Lithe as a cat, Clay stretched, and the sheet slid down his hips. Meg rescued it before it slid any farther. "I'll scrub your back if you'll scrub mine," he offered.

Meg shook her head. Just the thought made her tremble. "The doctor says you're not to get up for a few more days. You've got to build up your strength. You were really sick, you know." Deftly, she draped the sheet around his waist. Clay immediately captured her hand and held it tightly.

"So everyone keeps telling me," he said a little wryly. "Particularly the doctor. He told me that if it weren't for you, I'd be in the hospital this minute." His eyes darkened, and the hand that held hers tightened. "Were you worried?" he asked softly.

"We all were," she answered as noncommittally as she could. She wasn't sure she wanted Clay to know just how frantic with worry she had been during that long, exhausting night when his fever had raged. She loosened her hand and began soaping his arm.

"I don't care about the others. I care about you. Were you worried?" he asked again. His voice was gruff.

"Well, of course I was," she began briskly. "You were my responsibility and—" Then something in his eyes forced her to speak the truth. "I was terrified," she confessed as his eyes probed hers. "Your fever was so high, and you couldn't seem to rest." Her voice broke. "It was one of the worst nights of my life."

"I'm sorry," he said softly. "I wish it hadn't happened."

Meg smiled a little weakly. "It was hardly your fault," she told him. "We'd better get on with this sponge bath, or you'll get a chill and be sick all over again."

"I could never get a chill around you," he told her with a meaningful smile on his face. "A fever, yes, but never a chill."

"I wouldn't be too sure of that," she said, deliberately ignoring the meaning of his words.

She rinsed his arm, then began to soap his chest. As

146

she dragged the washcloth across his strong muscles, she couldn't keep a little thrill of excitement from moving down her spine. Clay was so virile and manly that she had to resist the urge to run her fingers through the hair that covered his chest.

"Enjoying yourself?" he asked lazily as she rinsed away the soap.

Meg blushed wildly. She couldn't help it. She had been enjoying the feel of his hair-roughened skin beneath her hands. She just hadn't realized it was so obvious. She immediately snatched away the washcloth and busied herself with the towel.

"Don't be embarrassed," Clay told her. There was laughter in his voice. "I'm glad you like touching me. I enjoy touching you very much. Every time I see you, I want to touch you." His eyes were warm on her face.

Meg stared back speechlessly. She felt exactly the same way, but she didn't want him to know that.

"The other night was just the beginning," he told her. "We're going to have many, many more nights together, honey, and they won't be in the hayloft, either." He brushed her cheek with his hand.

Meg smiled a little tremulously, but she didn't say anything. To be honest, she didn't know what to say. Clay, however, misinterpreted her silence.

"You're not sorry we made love, are you, Meg?" he asked. His eyes were suddenly troubled.

Meg looked away. "No," she stammered. "It's just that . . ." Her voice trailed off awkwardly.

Clay looked more troubled than before. "There was no time to talk afterward," he said hoarsely. "But I could swear I didn't hurt you or frighten you. I thought you enjoyed it as much as I did."

"I—did," she finally managed to say. She stared down at his chest. "You were wonderful," she said in a voice that was pitched so low that he had to strain to hear it. "I'm just not used to talking about it."

147

The tension drained from his face, and he smiled tenderly. "Oh, my darling," he murmured. "I was afraid you regretted our lovemaking, and I wouldn't have that happen for the world."

Meg stole a look at him. "Never that," she returned softly. She was speaking the truth. No matter what happened between the two of them, she knew she would always remember that night. Clay had been forceful and tender, demanding and persuasive. He had been everything she had ever dreamed of.

He pulled her toward him. His lips sought and found hers. Meg leaned forward, feeling the dampness of his chest through her blouse. Slowly Clay coaxed her mouth open, forcing her to respond to him. When Meg finally pulled away, they were both breathing quickly.

"I'd like to pull you into bed with me and make love to you here and now." His eyes felt like satin on her face.

"I don't think you're in any condition for that," Meg murmured a little mischievously.

"Unfortunately, you're right," Clay told her. His voice was full of regret. "We'll have to wait until I get my strength back. And then I'll really make you blush." He chuckled delightedly at the confusion in her face.

Meg took hold of his other arm and quickly finished his sponge bath. Clay had a way of turning her inside out, she ruefully thought. As she patted him dry, she forced herself to be brisk and efficient. Mercifully, he seemed to be thinking of something.

"Is your aunt staying here tonight?" he asked as she was leaving the room.

Meg stopped and turned. "Yes, she is," she told him as she rested the bowl of water on the bookcase by the door. "She's been here every night. She does the cooking for the men while I look after you."

"Send her home," Clay ordered. He leaned back and closed his eyes a little wearily.

"But, Clay—" she protested.

148

"She can come back tomorrow, but send her home tonight." His voice was dictatorial, and Meg knew that when he was in that kind of mood, there was no use arguing with him.

"All right," she said a little helplessly. "But I don't see—"

"I want you all to myself," he interrupted. He opened his eyes and gazed at her intently. "I may not be able to take advantage of the situation, but at least we can be alone."

His words and the look on his face took her breath away. "All right," she whispered. She picked up the bowl of water and started out the door.

"Meg?" he asked, suddenly sounding like a forlorn little boy.

She half-turned. "Yes?"

"Hurry back."

She smiled gently. "I will."

That night, the house felt unusually quiet. Much to Meg's surprise, Helen had been glad to go home to her own bed.

"I'll be back in the morning, though," she promised Meg as she kissed her good night.

Meg hugged her gratefully. "I don't know what we'd have done without you," she told her aunt.

"You'd have managed." Though Helen spoke lightly, Meg could tell she was pleased. "Give Clay a good-night kiss for me," she threw over her shoulder as she left the house.

Meg laughed a little breathlessly. "That's something I'll let you do for yourself," she called after her aunt. She watched Helen drive off, wondering just how much she knew or guessed about Meg's relationship with Clay.

"How do you feel?" she asked Clay a few minutes later. She turned on the light by his bed, then fiddled with his covers. Even though she knew it was ridiculous, she was feeling a little nervous now that they were finally alone.

"I'm tired," Clay murmured sleepily. "You really wore me out with that sponge bath. How about you?"

"I'm a little tired, too," she confessed. Nursing Clay wasn't easy.

"Meg," he said in a voice filled with urgency. "Come to bed with me."

She took a step backward. "Don't be silly," she said feebly. "You're in no condition to . . ." Her voice trailed off.

He chuckled. It was a rich, warm, intimate sound, and it filled the room. "Actually, there's nothing I'd rather do than make love with you. But you're right. I'm in no condition. Come to bed with me anyway. If we can't do anything else, at least we can sleep together."

"You'd get a better night's sleep alone," Meg told him.

"I doubt that. Don't you know that I dream about you every night and I toss and turn wishing you were beside me? No, the only way I'll get a good night's sleep is if you're here with me."

Meg stopped protesting. She didn't really want to protest anyway. "I'll go get ready for bed," she said.

Clay smiled at her and closed his eyes contentedly.

As she slipped into her nightgown and went through the mechanics of washing her face and brushing her teeth, her heart pounded and her hands shook. Just the thought of being so close to Clay gave her goosebumps.

She slipped quietly into his room and turned off the light. Clay seemed to be asleep. She stood hesitantly beside his bed, wondering what to do. Perhaps it would be better if she simply went back to her own room.

"Take that thing off," Clay said abruptly.

"What thing?" she asked, startled.

"That thing you're wearing. I want to feel you, all of you, next to me." In the moonlight, his eyes were commanding.

150

Meg slowly lifted her arms and pulled the gown over her shoulders. It fell in a heap around her feet. At least the light was off, she thought. She didn't realize how brightly the moonlight illuminated the room until she heard Clay draw in his breath sharply.

"You're beautiful," he said simply.

He held out his arms, and Meg felt herself move slowly toward him. When she reached the bed, he took hold of her. For a minute, he ran his hands down her body.

"Exquisite torture," he murmured as he pulled her under the covers.

He immediately turned her so that she faced him. Meg slipped an arm under his head and held him tenderly.

"You promised to sleep," she reminded him.

"I know I did," he said regretfully. "But right now, I have to admit, I'm not very interested in sleeping. I'm more interested in you."

"But, Clay—" she started to protest.

"No talking," he commanded. "We can talk tomorrow." His hand moved down to the silken curve of her breast. "Now I want you to kiss me."

Meg touched his forehead with her lips.

"Not like that," he growled. "Like this."

He pulled her to him, pressing the curves of her body against the hard contours of his body. His lips found hers and, as they did so, Meg felt her common sense slip away under the intoxicating influence of his mouth. She loved the feel of him against her, loved the way her body responded to his. It wasn't until she felt him shudder that she remembered where they were and why.

"Clay, we really shouldn't," she told him gently.

She felt him relax and knew what it cost him to ease his hold on her.

"I know," he said. There was passion in his voice. "But you can't blame me for wanting to make love to you. Every night I dream about you, every night I remember what it was like when I possessed you."

151

"I think about it, too," Meg confessed a little shyly. "But let's not rush things. Let's wait until you're well."

"Unfortunately, I don't think I can do anything *but* wait," he told her ruefully. "I'm too tired and weak." He was quiet for a moment before he spoke again. "You'll wait for me, won't you, Meg?"

"I'll wait," she promised.

She cuddled up beside him, thrilling as she felt the long lines of his body pressed against hers. She was sure she'd lie awake all night, just listening to the sounds of her heart and Clay's rhythmic breathing. But a few moments later, they were both sound asleep.

CHAPTER NINE

"Henry just called," Meg said as she walked into the kitchen where her aunt was busily making pies. Her face was troubled.

Helen turned and looked at her. "Henry?" she asked blankly.

That made Meg smile. Only a few months earlier, Helen had been urging Meg to marry Henry. Now she didn't seem to recognize his name.

"Henry Johnson," she said patiently. "The lawyer from Houston who asked me to marry him."

"Oh, him," Helen said. She turned back to her pie. "What did he want?"

"He wants me to have dinner with him this evening." The troubled look was back on Meg's face. "I said I would, but I'm a little worried about leaving Clay. You know how he likes to have someone with him all the time."

There was more to it than that, although Meg didn't say so to her aunt. Clay had been very possessive lately, and she was afraid he wouldn't understand why she felt she had to see Henry.

"I know he likes to have *you* with him all the time,"

Helen said dryly. "I don't know how he'll feel about someone else. But if it makes you feel any better, I'll stay this evening until you get back. I won't be his first choice, but at least he won't be alone."

Meg's face lit up. "You're an angel," she said gratefully.

With sure hands, Helen began rolling out a piecrust. "Why are you having dinner with Henry anyway?" she asked. "I thought you turned him down when he asked you to marry him." She put down her rolling pin and began lifting the crust into the pan.

"I did. But he's never really taken no for an answer," Meg explained. "I think he was really surprised when I said no."

"You did go out with him for over a year," Helen reminded her.

"I know. And that's why I think I owe it to him to have dinner with him tonight. I want to make it clear to him once and for all that I haven't changed my mind. Otherwise"—her voice faltered, then grew stronger—"otherwise, when I go back to Houston in two weeks, he'll want to pick up where we left off. I don't want that, not for his sake and not for mine."

"Are you going back to Houston in two weeks?" Helen asked a little wistfully. She kept her eyes on the second crust she was rolling out as she spoke.

"I have to," Meg answered, trying to keep her voice from sounding as unhappy as she felt. She didn't want to go back to Houston. With every fiber of her being, she wanted to stay at Broken Rock. But she couldn't forget her fears, her fears that Clay's passion for her was only a temporary thing. Each day, those fears were growing stronger, and Clay had done nothing to alleviate them. "My agreement with Clay was only for three months. Jake is expecting me back at La Bonne Femme, and I'm scheduled to start taping some new TV shows after I get back."

"You seemed so happy here," Helen said. The regret in her voice was obvious. "I've been hoping you'd stay."

"I have been happy here," Meg told her gently. "But you don't want me to be Clay's cook for the rest of my life." Or until he gets tired of me, she added silently to herself.

"No, of course not. But I just couldn't help wishing . . ." Her voice trailed off.

Meg knew exactly what her aunt had been wishing. She'd been wishing exactly the same thing.

"We still have two weeks before I have to leave," she told her aunt as cheerfully as she could. It wasn't much comfort, but it was the best she could do.

Her aunt brightened visibly. "You're right. And who knows what will happen in two weeks?"

Meg looked at her aunt, then took a deep breath. "Aunt Helen," she began, "if you're hoping Clay will fall in love with me and propose in the next two weeks, I'm afraid you're going to be disappointed. He enjoys my company, he likes having me here, but I don't think he's in love with me."

"But you're in love with him, aren't you?" her aunt asked shrewdly. "I don't want to pry," she said quickly, when Meg didn't answer. "That's why I haven't pressed you about it. But since you brought it up—"

"I brought it up because I don't want you to be disappointed when I go back to Houston. Clay's an old friend," she told Helen steadily, "nothing more. I came out to the ranch because he needed a cook and I needed a break. Don't read any more into it than that," she pleaded with her aunt. "If you do, I'm afraid you're going to be disappointed."

Before Helen could answer, there was a knock at the back door. Meg hurried over to open it with a feeling of relief. She'd had about as much of this conversation as she could take.

155

"Good morning, Dr. Brandt," she said as she pulled open the door.

"Good morning, Meg. Good morning, Helen. How's the patient?" he asked.

"Much better," Meg told him. "I think you're going to be pleased."

"Good." Dr. Brandt sniffed the air appreciatively. "Is that blueberry pie I smell baking?"

Helen smiled. "It is, and it should be ready to eat by the time you've finished with Clay."

"I do love warm pie," Dr. Brandt said as he moved toward the door leading out of the kitchen. "I can find my own way," he told Meg as she started to go with him. "You stay here and visit with your aunt."

"You certainly do know the way to his heart," Meg observed as the doctor left the kitchen. "I thought at first he was coming out here every day for Clay's sake. But now I think he's been coming just so he can eat your cooking."

Helen merely laughed. "Why don't you give me a hand with these dishes," she said.

Together they cleaned up the kitchen and planned the meals for the next couple of days. Helen had just put out a large slice of blueberry pie when Dr. Brandt came back into the kitchen.

"Clay wants you," he said immediately to Meg. He winked at her. "In fact, he's champing at the bit. He's got some good news for you."

"What is it?" she asked.

"I'll let him tell you," he answered. "I don't know how you've done it," he added as Meg dried her hands. "I wouldn't have thought anything or anyone could keep Clay Beaumont in bed for a week. You must be a mighty good nurse."

Meg merely smiled. She didn't wait to hear any more. She hurried up the stairs to Clay's room, where she found him sitting up in bed looking extraordinarily pleased with

156

himself. She stopped in the doorway for a moment and stared at him. His illness hadn't taken its toll on his magnificent body. His torso and shoulders were as muscular and rugged as ever. He certainly didn't look like a man who had spent nearly a week in bed, she thought.

"The doctor says you've got good news," she said as she entered the room.

Clay gave her a huge smile. "He says I can get up today," he said. "It's a good thing, too. I don't think I could have taken another day in bed—not even with you for a nurse."

"That's wonderful!" she exclaimed.

"The first thing I'm going to do is take a long, hot shower. After that, who knows?" He gave her such a sexy grin that Meg felt herself blush.

"You don't want to overdo," she said quickly, "or you'll end up right back in bed."

"Right back in bed is where I intend to end up," he told her wickedly, "with you beside me. The last couple of nights I haven't felt like doing anything but sleeping. Tonight is going to be different. It's going to be our night." His silvery eyes captured hers, and Meg felt herself staring back at him helplessly. Her heart sank to her shoes. Why had Henry called today of all days, and why had she agreed to have dinner with him?

"I've got something to tell you about tonight," she said finally breaking through the tension.

"We'll have steak for dinner," Clay said, interrupting her, "a big thick steak. And a bottle of good red wine. I don't want any more of that sickroom food."

"All right," Meg said unhappily. "But there's something I have to tell you." She took a deep breath. "I won't be here for dinner."

Clay's face grew dark. "Oh," he said ominously. "Just where will you be?"

"I'll be having dinner with an old friend," she said with a gulp.

157

Clay's eyes grew frosty. "Couldn't you cancel it?" he asked.

"I'd like to," Meg told him, "but—"

"But what?" Clay demanded. "Who is this old friend?"

"Henry Johnson," Meg told him. "I wouldn't have agreed to have dinner with him," she rushed on, "if I'd known you'd be able to get up."

"Henry Johnson?" Clay repeated. His voice was soft but angry. "Isn't he the man your aunt told me about? The one who asked you to marry him?"

She nodded miserably.

"And you'd rather have dinner with him than with me!" Clay's voice was beginning to gain strength.

"Of course, I wouldn't!" Meg cried. She was starting to get a little upset herself. "If you'll just be quiet a minute and let me explain—"

He cut her off almost at once. "I don't see that there's anything to explain. Either you spend the evening with him or with me. Make your choice."

"It isn't like that," she tried to tell him.

"Then why are you going out with him?"

"Because I owe it to him," Meg snapped. She was suddenly angry. Clay's behavior wasn't making any sense to her. Surely he wasn't jealous? It seemed incomprehensible to her that Clay could be jealous of anyone.

"You owe it to him," Clay replied quietly. "Don't you owe me anything?"

"No, I don't. Not the way you mean it," she replied evenly. Then she took a deep breath. She felt she had to try one last time to make Clay see reason. "Try to understand," she said, curbing her temper as best she could. "I'd much rather be here with you, but I've already told Henry I'd see him and I don't feel I can back out now. I dated him for over a year," she added a little desperately. "I think he's entitled to a little consideration."

Clay's eyes were cold, so cold that Meg felt a shiver.

"It seems to me that you still have some feeling for this Henry Johnson," he told her.

"No, I don't," she protested.

"Then why the hell are you going out with him?" Clay yelled.

"You're jealous," Meg said suddenly. Nothing else could account for his behavior.

"Jealous?" he asked. He stood up abruptly.

Meg gasped, and the color rushed to her face as her eyes moved involuntarily down his body. Clay was stark naked—and sensational. He began to move toward her, and Meg felt herself tense.

"You're damned right I'm jealous," he told her grimly. "I told you that night in the hayloft that you belong to me now, and I meant it."

"I don't belong to anyone," Meg said defiantly.

"That's where you're wrong," Clay said menacingly. "You're mine, and I don't intend to share you."

"You're being ridiculous!" Meg burst out. "You don't own me!"

"Don't I?" he asked softly. "We'll see about that."

The look on his face alarmed her. She began backing toward the door, but Clay's long arm reached over her shoulder and slammed it shut. He grasped her arms with his hands.

"What does Henry Johnson have that I don't have?" he asked hoarsely.

As Clay pulled Meg closer to him and she began to feel the heat from his body, her heart started to pound.

"Nothing," she whispered weakly.

Clay's arms encircled her, and he crushed her to him. With fierce hunger, his lips descended to hers. It was a devastating kiss, one that ignited little fires up and down her body.

"Does he make you feel like this?" Clay demanded. His voice was thick. "Does he make your heart pound and your body clamor for more?"

Meg pulled away. She *had* to put a stop to this before things got completely out of hand. Slowly she raised her hand to her lips and touched them gently.

"They're swollen," Clay told her, watching the movement with fevered eyes. "Swollen with the desire *I* make you feel. Come to bed with me now," he urged her.

Meg's eyes grew wide. "No," she cried involuntarily. "Not like this."

"Why not?" he demanded. "I'll make you forget Henry Johnson and every other man you've ever met."

"You're angry," she said. "We're both upset. Making love isn't going to solve anything."

"You might be surprised," he told her. He reached for her again, but Meg sidestepped him.

"Dammit, Meg," he burst out before he could stop himself. "Can't you see how much I need you, how much I want you?" He wanted to tell her that he was afraid of losing her again, but he couldn't. Not while she was standing there telling him that she was going out with another man.

"Yes," she said quietly, "I can."

He wanted her, he needed her, but he didn't love her, she thought. There was a dull ache in her heart that was growing stronger with every passing moment.

"I'm having dinner with Henry to tell him I can't see him again," Meg went on. "I'll be back early, and if you're awake—"

"I will be," he interjected.

"If you're still awake," she went on resolutely, "we'll talk."

"Talk, hell," he muttered.

Meg left him standing in the middle of the room. For the rest of the day, she saw nothing of him. He got dressed and went into his den to catch up on some work, and he remained there all day. To make matters worse, Meg developed a headache that aspirin wouldn't cure.

160

She knew it was a tension headache. It couldn't be anything else.

It would have been much easier to call Henry and cancel their dinner. She would have been happy, and Clay would have been happy, too. Why hadn't she done it, then? She didn't know, though she supposed it had something to do with her pride and her desire for some kind of commitment from Clay. A commitment he obviously couldn't or wouldn't make. Clay wanted her, he was almost greedy for her body and her lovemaking, she thought uncomfortably, but he wasn't offering any bond of permanence or stability. Henry, on the other hand, wanted marriage and children.

Meg sighed. She took two aspirin, put a damp cloth over her eyes, and took a nap, trying not to feel trapped by Clay's anger or her own stubbornness. She wished the evening were over.

When Henry came to pick her up, Clay was waiting in the living room.

"Bring her home early," he ordered as his cold eyes raked over the other man.

Henry murmured something and tried to hurry Meg out the door.

"I'll be waiting up," Clay reminded her ominously.

"He's somewhat autocratic, isn't he?" Henry asked indignantly as they left the ranch.

"He's been sick," Meg said lamely. Clay hadn't behaved very well.

"Does that give him the right to order you around like that?" Henry wanted to know.

"Well, I do work for him," she pointed out.

"And I've never understood why," he grumbled. "You could have had your choice of jobs in Houston. Why you chose to bury yourself out here in the sticks for three months is beyond me."

"I like it out here in the sticks," Meg said coolly.

161

At the tone of her voice, Henry smiled apologetically. "I'm sorry. I forgot that you grew up on one of these ranches. Look, let's forget about Beaumont for the rest of the evening."

That would be impossible for Meg to do. She stared miserably at the scenery as it flashed by. She wished more than ever that she had never agreed to see Henry. Seeing him was a mistake in more ways than one. Why, oh why hadn't she told him over the phone? Now she had to have dinner with him when all she wanted was to be at Broken Rock with Clay.

Henry was a nice man and would make some woman a good husband, but compared with Clay . . . She sighed dispiritedly. Nobody could compare with Clay. That was the trouble.

As soon as they had eaten, she told Henry in the most tactful words she could think of that she couldn't see him again. He took the news well, so well that Meg decided he had been expecting it.

"I suppose you think you're in love with Clay Beaumont," he said as they started back to the ranch.

"Clay is an old friend," Meg answered evasively.

"I suppose any woman would feel the same way," Henry mused. "He's an exciting man. But he'll never marry you," he told her. "From everything I've heard and read, I'd have to say he's not the marrying kind."

Unfortunately, Meg agreed with him, but she wasn't going to admit that to Henry. She wasn't even going to discuss Clay with Henry. She was about to change the subject when a strange thumping sound caught her attention.

"What's that noise?" she asked as Henry pulled the car over to the side of the road.

"It sounds like a flat tire," Henry said glumly.

Meg's heart sank. At this rate it would be another hour before she got back to the ranch.

"I'll help you change it," she said briskly.

162

Henry shook his head. "I don't have a spare," he said even more glumly. "We'll just have to sit here until someone stops."

Meg stared at him in consternation. "But that could take hours!" she cried. "I've got to get back to the ranch!"

"You can't walk," Henry pointed out irritably. "It's too far, and it's pitch black outside."

Meg bit her lip in exasperation. Henry was right. They were just about halfway between Morganville and Broken Rock, and there was nothing around them for miles.

"I'll put out a couple of flares," Henry said. "Maybe somebody will stop soon."

Even with the flares to signal their distress, it seemed like an eternity before anyone stopped to help. It was nearly one in the morning before she got home. As Henry pulled to a stop in front of the house, Meg's heart sank. Every light in the house was on. Clay was obviously waiting up.

"If you ever change your mind," Henry began as he walked her to the door.

"I know," Meg said gently. "And thank you, Henry. I'm sorry it didn't work out."

Henry leaned over to kiss her good-bye, and at that moment the porch light blazed into life and the door opened.

"Have you got any idea what time it is?" Clay demanded ferociously. He opened the screen door and pulled Meg inside. "Don't you ever show your face around here again," he told a flabbergasted Henry.

"Don't worry," Meg said to Henry, "I'll take care of this."

"But—" Henry began.

Clay slammed the door in his face. A moment later, Henry's car started.

"Some fiancé," Clay growled. "If anyone did that to me, I'd break the door down."

"He's not my fiancé," Meg said as Clay turned and started into the living room. She followed him. "Where's Aunt Helen?"

"She went home hours ago," he said curtly. "Where have you been? I thought you were going to be home early."

"We had a flat tire," Meg explained nervously. Clay obviously wasn't in the mood to be reasonable.

He chuckled bitterly. "That's the oldest excuse in the book. Surely you can come up with something better than that."

"It happens to be the truth," she said with dignity. She looked at Clay, and her heart fell to her feet. He looked about as approachable as a rattlesnake coiled to strike, and she knew her explanation would do no good whatsoever.

Then she rebelled. It was because of Clay that she had spent a miserable evening. Why should she have to explain anything? Why couldn't he simply trust her?

"I'm going to bed," she said angrily. Her dreams for them were turning to dust. "Maybe in the morning you'll be in a more reasonable frame of mind."

"Reasonable?" he asked incredulously. "Why should I be reasonable when you've been standing out on my front porch necking with another man?"

"We weren't—" Meg began, but then broke off abruptly. What was the use? "Good night," she said.

She turned and walked out of the room quickly. She didn't want him to see the hot tears that were suddenly spilling down her cheeks.

Clay stared after her, his face a mask of cold hard pride.

* * *

The next morning wasn't any better. Clay disappeared into his study and stayed there. Meg interrupted him only once, and that was to tell him he had a phone call.

"Oh," the woman said, sounding slightly nonplussed when Meg answered the phone. She obviously hadn't expected Meg to answer the phone. "Is this Broken Rock Ranch?"

"Yes, it is," Meg answered.

The woman's voice became a little stilted. "Will you tell Mr. Beaumont that Elaine is calling?"

"Just a moment, please," Meg said formally. She walked down to the study door and rapped on it. "You have a phone call," she called without opening the door.

Elaine. Where had she heard that name before? Then it came to her. Elaine was the clingy redhead Clay had brought with him that night he had stopped in at La Bonne Femme. She went back to the kitchen and attacked the breakfast dishes with a vengeance.

Thirty minutes later, Clay appeared, dressed in a light gray suit.

"I'm going into town," he announced.

Meg stared at him in consternation. "But, Clay," she protested, "you've been so sick. I don't think—"

"I feel fine," he interrupted. He glanced at his thin gold watch impatiently. "I won't be back at all tonight, so you needn't bother to wait up. I'll be spending the night in town."

Elaine, she thought instantly, and she felt as though she had been slapped in the face. She stared up at him. His eyes were hard and implacable.

Meg took a deep breath and swallowed her pride. "Don't go, Clay," she said quietly. "Stay here."

"Why should I?" he countered.

"Because I want you to," she answered simply.

Something flickered in his eyes. "I wanted you to stay here last night," he pointed out coldly. "But that didn't

165

seem to matter to you. Why should what you want matter to me?"

"Last night was different," Meg said. Keeping her voice steady was quite an effort.

"What makes last night so different?" Clay demanded angrily. "The fact that this Henry Johnson wants to marry you?"

"No," Meg said quietly, "I went out with Henry to tell him I couldn't see him again. You're going out with Elaine for an entirely different reason."

Clay ignored her last sentence. "That's why you *said* you were going out with him," he told her grimly. "But that wouldn't have taken until one in the morning."

"We had a flat tire," Meg said. "I told you that last night."

"And I didn't believe you," Clay flung back. "It doesn't take that long to put on a spare tire."

"Henry didn't have a spare," Meg said. Even as she spoke, she knew Clay wouldn't believe her.

He snapped. "You're going to have to do better than that," he said cynically. "Everyone has a spare tire."

Meg just stared at him. She wanted to plead with him not to go, not to throw away what they had, but something held her back. She'd already sacrificed enough pride.

"I told you why I went out with Henry," she said. "Why don't you tell me why you're going out with Elaine?"

He raised an eyebrow. "Why do you think?"

Meg felt the color drain from her face. It was all over between them, she thought. It was all over before it ever really had a chance to get started.

Clay stared at her white face and wide, shocked eyes. For a moment it seemed as though he would speak.

"I hope you have a nice time," she told him in a voice that was not her own. She turned and walked slowly out of the kitchen.

Clay stared after her for a moment, crushing the brim of his Stetson between his fingers. Then with a muttered oath he went out the back door, slamming it loudly behind him.

Clay didn't come home that night, and he didn't come home the next night either. When he finally did return to Broken Rock, he found Meg putting suitcases in her car.

"What's going on here?" Clay demanded.

"Just what it looks like," Meg said calmly. "I'm leaving."

"You can't leave yet. Your three months aren't up."

"Does it matter?" she asked wearily. "Under the circumstances, I would think you'd be happy to have me leave."

"Well, I'm not. We made an agreement, and I expect you to stick to it."

Meg finished putting her suitcases into the car. "It's over, Clay," she told him. "Whatever there was between us, and it couldn't have been much, is over. Let it go now while we each have a few pleasant memories."

"Pleasant memories," he echoed incredulously. "Is that all these past few weeks have been to you?"

Meg shrugged. "Some of them haven't even been that," she said evenly. She suddenly decided to put her cards on the table. "Look, Clay," she told him, "you brought me out here with one purpose and one purpose only—to get me into bed with you. Fool that I am, you succeeded. Let's leave it at that."

"What if I don't want to leave it at that?"

"I'm afraid you don't have much choice. You surely don't expect me to welcome you back with open arms after you've just spent two nights with one of your girl friends."

Meg got into the car before he could answer. She had spent last night and the night before in a flood of tears, and it had left her numb. Now she was glad for the numbness. It let her face Clay without breaking down completely.

"Do me a favor, Clay," she said quietly. "Next time you want to disrupt someone's life, find somebody else."

Without waiting for him to answer, she started the car and drove away.

She drove as far as her aunt's house. She would have preferred to drive on into Houston, but she knew she couldn't leave without spending one night at Helen's ranch. Her aunt would never forgive her if she rushed away without a proper good-bye.

"I still don't understand why you're going back to Houston," Helen said as they were having dinner.

"My producer had to move up the production of my show," Meg explained patiently. "He needs me back in town right away." She stared down at her uneaten plate of food. That explanation seemed like the best one under the circumstances. She could hardly tell Helen the truth.

"I'm sure Clay was disappointed when you told him you were leaving," Helen said. "He likes having you around almost as much as I do."

Meg lifted her shoulders noncommittally. "He understands why I left," she said briefly. She put her fork down. She couldn't pretend to eat another bite, not even for her aunt's sake.

Helen noticed at once. "You haven't eaten anything," she said anxiously. "I hope you're not going to be sick."

Only sick at heart, Meg thought. "I'm just a little nervous about getting back to the grind," she said aloud. "A TV show is more work than you'd think."

"I'm sure it is," Helen agreed. She began collecting the dishes. "You go in the living room and relax for a few minutes. I'll bring in dessert, and we'll have a nice long talk."

A nice long talk was the one thing Meg didn't want, particularly if her aunt insisted on talking about Clay.

"I'm a little tired," she began.

168

"I won't keep you up long," her aunt promised.

For just a little while, then I can escape to my room and be alone with my misery, Meg told herself as she sat down on the sofa.

"I've got a confession to make," Helen said after she had cut Meg a slice of apple pie and poured her a cup of coffee. "It's about you and Clay."

"That sounds very dramatic," Meg said lightly. She put the pie on the table in front of her and took a sip of the coffee. It was hot, strong, and bracing—just what she needed if her aunt insisted on talking about Clay.

Helen gave her a troubled look. "I've worried about this all summer," she told Meg. "I just couldn't decide what to do. Then this morning, when you called to say you were going back to Houston, I knew I had to tell you."

Meg put down her coffee cup and leaned forward. The look on her aunt's face frightened her. "Whatever it is," she said gently, "it can't be that bad."

"At the time it didn't seem bad at all," Helen said sadly. "In fact, at the time it seemed like a very good idea. Now I see just how wrong we were. I just hope you can forgive your uncle and me."

Meg saw that her aunt's eyes had filled with tears. She got up and moved to the sofa beside her. "You and Uncle John always had my best interests at heart," she told her aunt. "I know that. What could you possibly have done that I wouldn't forgive?"

What was all this about? she was wondering. Why was her aunt so upset? She took Helen's hand in her own and began to pat it.

Helen took a deep breath.

"Your uncle and I were very worried about you that summer you were dating Clay," Helen said. "We loved Clay, of course. He was like a son to us. But you were our daughter, and you were so very young."

169

"I don't understand what you're trying to say," Meg told her aunt gently.

Helen gave her a weak smile. "Of course you don't. I'll try to explain it a little more clearly. We realized that you had fallen in love with Clay," she told her niece. "And that worried us. But we were even more worried when we learned that Clay had fallen in love with you."

Meg stared at her aunt incredulously. "How in the world did you get the idea that Clay had fallen in love with me?" she asked.

"From Clay," her aunt answered simply. "He came to us one day and told us he was going to ask you to marry him."

Meg was speechless. Now it was Helen's turn to pat Meg's hand.

"You were only eighteen," Helen went on, "and you were so obviously in love. We knew that you'd quit school and marry Clay at once."

"Would marrying Clay have been so bad?" Meg asked faintly.

Helen shrugged tiredly. "Who knows? At the time we thought it would. Clay's reputation with women left a lot to be desired, and you were little more than a child. We just didn't see how it could work. So we asked Clay to wait, to give you a little more time to grow up before he said anything. If you two were still in love after a year or so, we told Clay we'd gladly give our consent to your marriage."

Meg got up, walked over to the window, and stared blankly into the night.

"Clay argued with us, of course," Helen went on. "He told us over and over that waiting wouldn't make any difference." Her voice fell. "I'm ashamed to say that we reminded him of everything John had ever done for him, of how much he owed us. In the end he agreed to wait."

Meg turned to face her aunt. Helen was looking at her pleadingly, as if begging her to understand.

"You went back to college, and we never heard you mention Clay again. Naturally, we thought we had saved you from a marriage that would never have worked. Now I'm not so sure. Every time I saw you and Clay this summer, I was struck by how right you were together. John and I shouldn't have interfered, and I bitterly regret that we did."

Meg pulled herself together. She went back to the sofa and dropped down beside her aunt.

"You and Uncle John did what you thought was right," she told her aunt comfortingly. "No one can blame you for that."

"Then you don't hate us for what we did?"

"Of course not," Meg said reassuringly. "I was in love with Clay that summer, and he may have thought he was in love with me. But that doesn't mean we would have gotten married and lived happily ever after. You know what Clay's like. He enjoys women. He always has, and he always will. It wouldn't have been long before someone else came along who caught his fancy."

It was breaking her heart to say these things, to know that once upon a time she and Clay had had a chance at happiness together.

"Hasn't Clay ever said anything about this to you?" Helen asked curiously. "I thought he might have told you about it this summer."

Meg thought of the evening she and Clay had picnicked down by the stream. That night he had seemed to be holding something back, but she hadn't expected it to be something like this.

"No," she said aloud. "He's never said a word."

"I don't suppose he would," Helen said absently. "He's far too honorable for that."

Meg got to her feet. Her head was beginning to ache. "I think I'll go to bed," she said.

Her aunt looked at her anxiously. "You are looking a little tired," she commented. "Perhaps you should get

171

some sleep. But before you go, there's one more thing I want to tell you."

"Is it about Clay?" Meg asked wearily. She didn't think she could bear to hear anything more about Clay. Reluctantly, she sat back down beside her aunt.

"Just after your uncle died, I discovered he had run up a lot of debts. They were nothing unusual," she hastened to reassure her niece, "and they wouldn't have been a problem if John had been alive. But once he was gone, I didn't know how I'd pay back all the money we owed."

"You should have come to me," Meg said gently. "I would have helped you."

Helen smiled at her niece. "You couldn't have done anything but worry, and I was worried enough for both of us."

"I have some money saved," Meg began.

"It wouldn't have been nearly enough," Helen told her. "And I wouldn't have felt right taking it." Her voice grew a little more brisk. "The week after you went back to Houston, Clay came to see me, and I told him everything. I hadn't meant to, but he guessed something was wrong."

Meg was looking at her in consternation. Clay had told her a different version of this story.

"Clay immediately got out his checkbook and wrote me a check for the whole amount," Helen went on. "I tried to refuse, but he insisted." Her voice dropped. "He said he owed it to me for all John had done for him when he was young. So I took it."

Meg's consternation was growing, and so was her bitterness. This meant that her aunt's debts had been paid long before Clay had even approached her. There had never been a bank loan, and her aunt had never been in any danger of losing her home. Clay had come to her with a story designed to get her out to Broken Rock and into his bed. He had known what he wanted, and he had gone after it ruthlessly.

172

"That was very kind of Clay," she said in what she hoped was a normal tone of voice. Her aunt must never know what had happened between Clay and her.

"Yes," her aunt agreed. "He's a good man. That's why I hoped you and he—" She looked at her niece hopefully.

"No," Meg said firmly.

Her aunt sighed. "The two of you seem so right together."

Meg just shook her head. She didn't think she could take any more. She stood up determinedly. "I really have to get some sleep," she said.

"You're as white as a ghost!" her aunt exclaimed. "I've upset you by telling you all this."

Again Meg shook her head. "No," she said. "I'm glad you told me. I'm just very tired."

She kissed her aunt good night and escaped to her room. Mechanically, she undressed and got ready for bed. All the while, she refused to think of Clay, refused to think of the things her aunt had told her.

When she had turned the light off, though, she pulled her knees up to her chest and sat rocking back and forth in misery.

CHAPTER TEN

I'm glad to be back, Meg told herself insistently every morning when she woke up in her apartment in Houston. But only a very small part of her believed that, while the rest of her ached to be at Broken Rock with Clay. But that could never be, and Meg knew it.

To fill her days and nights, Meg threw herself into her work. When she wasn't actually working at La Bonne Femme or taping a TV show, she spent hours creating new menus and new recipes.

Clay called the day after her return to Houston. She picked up her phone expecting it to be her aunt, her employer, a friend welcoming her back—anyone but Clay. She very nearly hung up when she heard his voice, and later she wished she had. Just hearing him speak hurt her.

"Good morning, Meg," he drawled.

For a moment, it sounded to Meg as though there were a shade less assurance in his voice. But that was probably just the connection, she thought to herself. She had never known Clay to be unsure of himself, and she could think of no reason for him to start now.

"What can I do for you?" she asked crisply. The hand

holding the phone began to tremble. Why couldn't he leave her alone?

"You can come back out to the ranch," he returned quickly. "The men miss you."

She didn't answer. She couldn't. Tears had filled her throat.

"It's not the same without you here," he went on. "Even the house feels different."

"I'll give you the name of a good employment agency," Meg replied coolly once she got her emotions under control. "I'm sure they'll send out someone to replace me."

"No one could take your place," Clay told her softly. "We need you—I need you." The last three words seemed to have been torn out of him.

She closed her eyes. How many times had she heard that before? "I'm very busy," she said wearily. "I should have left the apartment five minutes ago."

"I'm busy, too," he burst out angrily. I should be on my way to a meeting with the governor right now."

"Then I'll say good-bye," Meg told him. "I wouldn't want to keep you."

"Dammit, Meg!" Clay roared. His voice was so loud, she had to hold the phone away from her ear. "Don't be like this! We need to talk!"

"We do *not* need to talk!" she yelled back. "We don't have anything to say to one another!"

"I don't believe that." His voice grew silken. "Please have dinner with me tonight. We'll straighten everything out."

Meg didn't hesitate. "I'm working tonight," she said coldly.

"Tomorrow night, then."

"I'm working tomorrow night, and the next night, and the next night," she told him. "In fact, as far as you're concerned, I'm working every night." Her voice turned a little desperate. "There's nothing for us to discuss, Clay. We've already said it all."

"You're wrong," Clay told her. "I have a great deal to say to you."

"That doesn't mean I have to listen," she countered. "As a matter of fact, I have no intention of listening to you ever again."

"I won't give up," Clay promised her. "I'll get you back in my life somehow."

Meg suddenly lost her temper. "Stop it, Clay," she cried. "I don't want to hear this. You got me out to Broken Rock under false pretenses, and once I was there, you seduced me. You lied to me, you used me, and then when things didn't go exactly your way, you disappeared for two nights with one of your girl friends." She took a deep breath. "I can't think what else you want from me —unless you want to ruin my life completely."

There was a stunned silence at the other end of the phone.

"I didn't lie to you," Clay finally said. His voice sounded strained. "And I certainly didn't use you."

"Don't play the innocent with me," Meg snapped. "I know all about the money you loaned my aunt. You loaned it to her long before you even approached me."

"Was that so terrible?" he asked mildly.

"Yes," she told him. "You deliberately took advantage of the situation to get me out to Broken Rock and into your bed."

Clay was now as angry as she was. "Do you think that's all I wanted you for? A quick roll in the hay?"

Meg winced. "That's exactly what I think," she said evenly. "And now I want you out of my life. If you call me again, I'll just hang up, and I'll keep hanging up until you get the message." As she slammed the phone down, she could hear Clay swearing.

It had taken most of the morning just to calm down after that. Never again, she vowed to herself. Never again would she expose herself to such pain. Even the sound of his voice cut her to ribbons.

That afternoon, she changed her phone number. It didn't do any good, because Clay got her new number from her aunt. Next, Meg bought a telephone answering machine. It didn't stop Clay from calling, but at least she didn't have to talk to him.

The telephone calls continued for a week. Then, abruptly, they stopped. Clay had finally realized she meant what she said. But instead of feeling relieved, she felt even more empty.

The day after the phone calls stopped, Clay started sending her flowers. Every morning before she left for work, a delivery boy appeared at her door with a huge bouquet in his hands. One day it was red roses, the next day pink lilies, the next day white and yellow daisies. After the first day, Meg tried to refuse the flowers, but that confused the teen-age delivery boy so much that she ended up accepting them.

"Nobody ever refuses flowers," he told her. He looked at her as though she were weird. "My boss won't believe me if I tell him you wouldn't take them. I'll probably be fired."

Meg took the flowers and dropped them off at a nursing home that she passed on her way to the restaurant. Every morning, she did the same thing. Clay would give up sooner or later, she told herself. He had to!

She was sitting in the TV studio one morning, going over her notes for the cooking show when Linda, her eighteen-year-old assistant, came rushing in to tell her that Clay was in the next studio being interviewed for a news show.

Why was it, she wondered a little bitterly, that for seven years she had never run into Clay? For four of those years, she had been living and working in Houston, and, although she had read about him in the newspaper and heard people talk about him, she had never once seen him. Now, however, he seemed to be everywhere she went. If it weren't such a ridiculous idea, she would have suspected him of doing it deliberately.

"It's about that big oil deal he just pulled off," the girl was chattering, interrupting Meg's thoughts. "Imagine Clay Beaumont in the next studio," she added blissfully. "My friends will just die when I tell them."

Meg remembered seeing something about the oil deal in the newspaper. She hadn't read it, though. In fact, she had quickly turned the page.

"You know him, don't you?" Linda asked Meg, giving her an admiring look.

"I know him," Meg replied repressively. "Now, about the show—"

"I think he's just about the best-looking man I've ever seen," Linda went on dreamily. "Don't you think he's gorgeous?"

"I've never noticed," Meg said. "We've got a show to do, Linda. I suggest you concentrate on that, not on some oil executive in the next studio."

She saw that her sharp tone had hurt Linda's feelings. She put her hand on the girl's arm. "I'm sorry," she said. "I shouldn't have snapped at you. But this is only the second show we've done since I've been back, and I suppose I'm still a little nervous about it."

"You shouldn't be nervous," Linda said at once. "You're wonderful."

Meg laughed. That kind of talk was good for her ego. "Here's what we're doing today," she began.

They were deep in discussion when Clay walked into the studio. Linda saw him first, and she stopped talking in midsentence. Meg looked up a moment later. Her heart bounded, then fell.

He strode over to the spot where the two of them were sitting and, without waiting for an invitation, pulled up another chair and joined them.

"Good morning, Meg," Clay said. He stared at her as

178

though he hadn't seen her for months, as though he were starved for the sight of her.

"How did you get in here?" Meg asked coldly. His presence was doing strange things to her. She wanted to reach over and touch his face with her hand, to feel his rough, slightly abrasive skin under her fingers. She also wanted to get up and walk away. But this was her studio, her TV show. If anyone left, it would be Clay.

He raised his eyebrows. "I walked in, of course." He turned his attention to Linda. "Aren't you going to introduce us?" he asked Meg.

Meg made the introductions, all the time wondering how to get rid of him.

"Do you think you could find me a cup of coffee?" Clay asked Linda. "I'm mighty thirsty after that interview."

"Of course I can," Linda said. She immediately leaped to her feet and hurried off.

"What are you doing in here?" Meg asked, trying to hide her trembling voice. "This is a closed studio. Visitors aren't allowed while we're taping."

"I'm not just any visitor," he replied airily. "I happened to mention to the station manager that *Cooking with Meg* is one of my favorite shows, and he invited me to sit in on today's taping."

"I won't allow it," Meg said flatly.

Clay shook his head. "You'll find it awfully hard to get rid of me. Of course," he said thoughtfully, "you could throw a temper tantrum and refuse to go on. Isn't that what stars do when things aren't going their way? It wouldn't be very professional, though, and I imagine you pride yourself on being professional."

He was right. Meg did pride herself on being professional.

"Besides," he added in that same thoughtful tone, "I imagine it would give rise to a lot of unpleasant gossip if you refused to go on just because of me."

179

He was right about that, too. "All right," Meg said tiredly. "You can stay, but only this once." She began walking toward the set. Clay's voice stopped her.

"I told you that I wasn't going to give up," he said softly. "I miss you, Meg, and I need you." His voice was full of emotion. "I'll follow you to the ends of the earth if I have to. I'm not letting you walk out of my life now."

Meg turned to stare at him. "You don't have much choice," she replied icily.

The show was a nightmare. Linda, her mind obviously on their audience, missed cue after cue, leaving Meg to flounder several times while she waited for the right pan or the right ingredients to appear. When it was finally over, she hurried off to her dressing room intending to lock the door, if necessary, to keep Clay out.

When she got there, the first thing she saw was a huge bouquet of red roses sitting on her dressing table. They were from Clay, of course. She knew that at once. No one else would send her flowers. She dumped them into the wastebasket, picked up her pocketbook, and, without removing any of the makeup she wore for the camera, slipped out the side door. She couldn't bear the idea of seeing Clay again. She drove to the restaurant praying that he wouldn't turn up there as well.

She saw him in other places, though. One day she even ran into him in the produce department of her local grocery store. In his exquisitely cut dark blue suit and immaculate white silk shirt, he looked ridiculously out of place with a little wire basket dangling from his arm. Meg didn't think he'd ever been in a grocery store before in his entire life.

"What in the world are you doing here?" she asked in spite of herself. He was standing in front of a variety of lettuce, looking totally bewildered.

"I'm picking up a few things for dinner," he answered, giving her a smile that told her he was glad to see her.

"Do you mean to tell me you still haven't hired another cook?" Meg wanted to know.

"I've had three since you left," he told her ruefully. "None of them has been able to measure up to you. I told you, you're irreplaceable."

"Keep trying," Meg advised him. "I'm sure you'll find someone sooner or later." Though walking away from him was sheer torture, she began to move toward the deli section. Clay immediately abandoned the lettuce and followed her.

Meg ignored him as best she could until she had paid for her purchases and was standing outside in front of the store.

"What about the food you were supposedly in there to buy?" she asked him dryly.

He shrugged. "If you'll invite me to have dinner with you tonight," he said persuasively, "I won't have to buy anything."

"We've been through this before," Meg said evenly. "I'm working."

"You can't be working every night," Clay challenged.

Meg lifted her chin and gave him a defiant look. "Well, I am," she said. "And as far as you're concerned, I always will be." All at once, she was having a hard time controlling her voice. She felt like bursting into tears; she felt like throwing herself into his arms. She felt confused and miserable. Why couldn't he leave her alone!

"Meg," he began in a tortured voice.

She turned on him. "Stop doing this to me," she cried. Hot tears filled her eyes and threatened to spill down her face. "You said you didn't want to hurt me, but that's exactly what you're doing." Blindly, she snatched up her bag of groceries and hurried off to her car.

She didn't hear from him anymore after that. He finally seemed to have gotten the message, she told herself. Oddly enough though, she found no comfort in that fact. Instead, she even felt more miserable than ever.

181

Then, one dark, rainy September night, when she had been back in town for nearly a month, she left the restaurant feeling particularly tired and dispirited. Clay was becoming an obsession with her. From the back, nearly every tall, broad-shouldered man she saw on the street reminded her of him, and every time she played back her telephone answering machine, she found herself hoping he had called.

She stopped in the doorway of the restaurant, wishing it wasn't two o'clock in the morning, wishing she was back at Broken Rock. Then she squared her shoulders and told herself she'd feel better after a good night's sleep. She closed the door behind her and immediately noticed Clay's Cadillac. It was parked in front of the restaurant. As she stepped outside, he got out of the car and walked toward her.

"I'm taking you home," he said abruptly. He made no greeting; he wasn't even particularly courteous. He took her firmly by the arm and didn't let go of her until she was sitting inside the car.

Meg had thought of protesting, of telling him that she had no intention of going anywhere with him, but as soon as he touched her, she couldn't say anything. She had been wishing for him, and now that he was here, she saw no reason to deny herself the little comfort his presence brought her. She knew she'd despise herself in the morning for not walking away from him, but the morning was hours away. For now, it was wonderful just to have Clay near.

"What about my car?" she asked, more for the sake of form than anything else. She didn't care about her car any more than he did.

"You can pick it up in the morning," he replied indifferently.

When they reached her apartment, Clay followed her up the stairs, just as she had known he would. She didn't

182

bother to invite him in either, since he obviously had every intention of coming in no matter what she said.

When they were inside her apartment, Meg took off her raincoat, hung it in the closet, and turned to find Clay staring at her.

"Are you looking for anything in particular?" she asked quietly.

He gave her his crooked smile, the smile she had come to love. "No," he drawled in reply. "I just like to look at you. Do you mind?"

"As a matter of fact, I do," she told him. The look in his eyes was making her feel a little flustered. "You just saw me a couple of weeks ago. I haven't changed any since then."

"That's not true," he countered swiftly. "You're more beautiful than you were a few weeks ago, if that's possible. Besides, last time I saw you, I was too busy dodging shopping carts to get to look at you as much as I wanted."

"Well, you're certainly making up for it now," Meg murmured. She turned away from the scrutiny of his eyes and walked into the living room. Clay followed her. She busied herself by turning on a few lights and rearranging a few pillows. Clay stood in the doorway and watched.

"Would you like to sit down?" she asked finally.

He gave her a lazy smile and sat down on the sofa. In the bright light cast by a lamp, Meg saw that Clay's face was tired and drawn, and there were circles under his eyes. She felt a pang in her heart as she looked at him. Obviously the last few weeks hadn't been easy on him, either. She sat down on a chair across from him and stared fixedly at the picture that hung on the wall just behind his left shoulder. She couldn't bear to look at his face. It hurt too much to see him like this.

"Why don't you sit over here?" he asked, patting the sofa beside him.

"I'm comfortable where I am, thank you," she replied coolly.

"And you don't want to get too close to me," he added bitterly. "Is that it?"

"That's it," Meg told him evenly. She was beginning to wish he would go. She couldn't think of anything to say. After everything that had happened between them, casual conversation seemed out of place.

"This is a nice room," Clay said. He looked around him, although Meg got the idea that he didn't really notice what he saw.

"Thank you," she said politely. For the life of her, she couldn't think of anything to add.

Silence fell between them. It was a heavy, awkward silence, and the longer it lasted the more miserable Meg felt.

This was a mistake, she told herself as she glanced down at her watch. There was no comfort to be found in this, only a cold ache that was spreading through her like the flu. She should have said good-bye to him at the door. If she'd been firm enough, he would have had no choice but to leave.

"Would you like some coffee?" she finally asked. She looked at her watch more pointedly this time. Perhaps he'd take the hint and leave.

"I didn't come here for coffee," Clay told her. He suddenly seemed impatient, and a little of his impatience rubbed off on Meg.

"Well then, why did you come?" she asked, even though she knew what his answer would be.

"I came because of you," he replied swiftly.

Meg's eyes rested on his face for a moment, then moved back to the picture on the wall. "I'm afraid you're just wasting your time," she said wearily.

"For God's sake, Meg," he burst out. "Can't we at least talk about it, about us?"

"There is no us," she told him. "There never was, and

184

there never will be." Quickly she got to her feet and started toward the door. "You'd better go now," she said over her shoulder.

All at once, she wanted him out of her apartment. She didn't know how much more of this she could take, but she knew it wouldn't be long before she broke down completely. Already she could feel her self-control slipping away. She didn't want him to see her cry.

As she moved toward the door, Clay jumped to his feet and caught her by the wrist. With a quick movement, he turned her so that she had to face him.

"Is everything you ever felt for me really dead?" he demanded harshly. His fingers tightened around her wrist.

Meg dropped her eyes to his chest. The look on his face was making her ache. The tears she had been holding back filled her eyes.

Clay saw the tears, and his voice softened. "Let's sit down," he said, leading her back to the sofa.

Meg sat down. She really didn't have much choice. Clay was holding her hand as though he had no intention of ever letting her go again.

"Why won't you come back to the ranch with me?" he asked.

She shook her head and stared down at the sofa. "I can't," she told him.

"Why the hell not?" he burst out. His frustration was obvious. "Why do you insist on making us both so miserable?"

She looked up. If he wanted the truth, then he'd get it. Perhaps then he'd leave her alone with her misery. "I can't go back to the ranch with you," she cried, "because I love you too much. I can't live with you waiting for the time when you grow tired of me, wondering every morning if this will be the day you meet someone else." Her words seemed to reverberate in the silence which followed.

185

"You love me?" Clay asked after a long moment. His voice sounded dazed. Then it grew stronger. "You love me, and you were going to walk out of my life without telling me how you felt?"

"Why should I have told you?" Meg asked evenly. "What difference would it make?"

"It makes all the difference," he told her. There was a note in his voice she had never heard before. "I thought—" He broke off and began again. "Come back to the ranch with me," he urged her.

Meg tried to pull her hand away, but he still refused to let it go.

"I just told you—" she began angrily.

"Come back as my wife," Clay interrupted softly.

Meg felt an hysterical urge to burst out laughing. "Aren't you going a bit too far?" she asked. "You don't have to ask me to marry you just because you want to make love to me."

Much to her surprise, he grinned. "It would seem that I have to do exactly that," he said.

He let go of her wrist and began searching his pockets for something. Finally he pulled out a small box and tossed it into her lap.

She looked at him suspiciously.

"Open it," he commanded. His silvery eyes had turned a warm gray.

Meg picked up the box and lifted the lid. Inside was a ring with the biggest diamond she had ever seen.

"What is this?" she asked faintly. "The Kohinoor diamond?" She stared down at the enormous marquise diamond in stupefaction.

"Is it too big?" he asked worriedly. "If it is, we'll take it back and exchange it for anything you want."

"It's not that," she said a little helplessly. She closed the box and handed it back to him. "But Clay—"

"I'm not doing this properly, am I?" Clay asked ruefully. "You'll have to be patient. I've never proposed to a

186

woman before—at least, I've never proposed marriage," he amended wickedly.

He cupped her chin with his hand and tilted her head back. Meg stared at him wonderingly. His warm gray eyes were filled with light.

"Meg, my wonderful Meg, I've loved you since our first summer together. Would you do me the honor of becoming my wife?" There was warm, rich laughter in his voice.

"Are you serious?" Meg whispered. She was afraid to believe what she was hearing.

He smiled then. It was a gentle smile. "I've never been more serious in all my life."

Deftly he opened the ring box and slipped the enormous diamond on her finger. When Meg moved her hand slightly, the diamond flashed fire in the light from the lamp.

Meg wasn't looking at the ring, though. She was staring at Clay's face.

"I should have told you long ago how much I love you. What do you say, Meg? Will you marry me?"

Meg felt as though it were her birthday and she had just been given the world. "Yes," she said softly. "Yes, I will."

Clay leaned over and kissed her. When their lips touched, Meg could feel new tenderness flowing between them that took her breath away.

"Come closer, woman," Clay whispered a moment later. He pulled her over, and Meg nestled against him happily. When she was safely in the circle of his arms, she reached up and pressed her lips against his.

"I don't believe this is happening," she murmured.

He chuckled. "Neither do I. When I came here tonight, I expected you to say no."

Meg reached up and followed the lines of his face with her fingers. "There are so many things I don't understand."

187

"We can talk later," he told her firmly. "Right now I can think of better things to do."

"So can I," she murmured. She drew his mouth down to hers for a long, slow kiss. Meg gloried in the feel of his strong arms holding her close.

The kiss deepened until Meg felt the sweet languor that Clay was always able to produce steal over her.

"Clay," she whispered against his mouth.

He drew away slightly and gazed at her. His eyes were possessive and adoring, caressing and passionate.

"What is it, honey?" he asked.

"It's Elaine," she said, and her own eyes clouded. She hated asking but she had to know. "Did you—" She didn't even want to say the words.

Clay read her thoughts easily. "No," he told her seriously. "I didn't sleep with her. As a matter of fact, I didn't even see her. I spent those two nights at my apartment."

Meg sat up straight. She knew him well enough to know he was telling the truth. "But I thought—"

"I know you did, and I let you think it," he said ruefully. "Elaine called that day to invite me to a party. I turned her down, but I decided I had to get away from the ranch for a while. I was being eaten up by jealousy." His voice darkened. "You can't imagine how I felt when I discovered you and Henry kissing on my front porch."

"Oh, yes I can," Meg told him fervently. She knew how she'd feel if she ever found him kissing another woman. "But it was just a good-bye kiss. It didn't mean anything."

"I know. You tried to tell me that. I wanted to believe you, but I couldn't." His warm gray eyes searched her soft blue ones. "I've been every kind of fool there is. Can you forgive me, Meg?"

"There's nothing to forgive," she told him gently.

"Yes, there is. When you jumped to the conclusion that

188

I was going to town to see Elaine, I let you think it. It was a childish thing to do, and I'm not very proud of it."

"I'm not particularly proud of some of the things I've done in the past, either," she told him slowly. "Do you remember that letter I sent you when I got back to college all those years ago?"

"Do I remember it?" he interjected a little savagely. "I couldn't forget it. It's haunted me for years."

"I made up the part about being pinned to a fraternity man," Meg said. It was painful for her to admit this. "I wanted to hurt you, to get back at you for rejecting me. If I hadn't—" She took a deep breath. "So you see, we both have things to forgive and forget."

Clay stared at her. "I didn't reject you," he told her. "That was the last thing I wanted to do. But—"

"I know," Meg said quickly. "Aunt Helen told me all about it."

Clay reached for her and pulled her back into the circle of his arms. "Come back here," he said. "I don't like having you so far away. When I got your letter," he went on, "I went a little crazy. I couldn't believe what I was reading, but there it was in black and white. I started dating as many women as I could, trying to find someone to take your place. But there wasn't anyone who could make me forget you."

Meg stirred in his arms. "I'm sorry," she said a little helplessly. "If I could go back, if I could undo the past—"

He stopped her words with a kiss. "It doesn't matter anymore. It's over. From now on we're going to think about the future."

"That sounds like a good idea to me," Meg murmured as she relaxed against him. She looked up. The expression on his face revealed his need for her. "I've always loved you," she said simply. "And I always will."

"Say that again," he asked. His hands framed her face so that he could watch her as she spoke.

"I'll always love you," she repeated. She stared up at him, her heart in her eyes.

"And I'll always love you," he vowed.

He found her soft eager lips, and as their kiss grew in intensity, Clay's embrace tightened until it drove the breath from her body.

"I think we'd better be married as soon as possible," he muttered hoarsely a few moments later. "What about tomorrow?"

Meg laughed softly. "I can't arrange a wedding that quickly."

"You may not be able to," he told her, "but I can."

She leaned back in his arms and gazed up at him. He held her as though she were some priceless treasure.

"I'd like a church wedding. A small church wedding. Even you might find that hard to arrange in a day," she said teasingly.

She remembered the dream that had shown her she couldn't marry Henry. Now, she thought blissfully, she would be marrying the right man, for the right reasons.

"Next week, then," he said firmly. "I refuse to wait any longer than that."

"You won't have to," she promised. "I don't want to wait any longer than that either." She cradled his head in her arms.

"What about a honeymoon?" he asked. "Where would you like to go? Paris—London—Hong Kong?"

She shook her head. "It doesn't matter to me where we go as long as we're together. You decide."

"In that case," he said with a silvery gleam in his eyes, "I think we should take a long cruise. We'll have nothing to do all day but stay in our stateroom and make love. We won't even have to get up for meals. The steward can bring them to us."

Meg couldn't help blushing at the thought. "That seems a little obvious to me," she protested. "Everyone will know what we're doing."

"So what?" he asked imperturbably. He searched her glowing blue eyes. "That's the whole purpose of a honeymoon. We'll have to spend a lot of time in bed if you're going to come home pregnant."

"Pregnant?" She was startled. "Aren't you rushing things a little?" The look in his eyes was slowly and surely warming her.

"I'm just making up for lost time," he replied. "And speaking of lost time, I hope you don't mind if we practice for the honeymoon."

Meg peeked up at him. "What do you mean?" she asked innocently, although she had a very good idea of what he meant.

Clay glanced eloquently toward the bedroom door. "We could wait, if you're rather, but—"

He buried his mouth in her neck, then slowly worked his way up to her lips. Meg gasped as the electricity sparked between them, then she let a sensual fog envelop her.

"It is getting late," she murmured breathlessly. "I'd hate to send you out into the dark."

"Then don't," he said succinctly.

Meg laughed and reached up to turn off the light.

"For once, we're going to do this properly." Clay stood up with Meg in his arms and strode toward the bedroom. As they entered the room, he kicked the door shut behind them.

Outside, the night sky had changed to gray, then silver, then gold. But it went unnoticed by the two lovers, who by that time were lost in their own magic night.

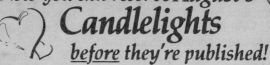

Now you can reserve August's Candlelights before they're published!

♥ You'll have copies set aside for *you*
  the instant they come off press.
♥ You'll save yourself precious shopping
  time by arranging for *home delivery.*
♥ You'll feel proud and efficient about
  organizing a system that *guarantees* delivery.
♥ You'll avoid the disappointment of not
  finding *every* title you want and need.

ECSTASY SUPREMES $2.75 each

☐ 133 SUSPICION AND DESIRE, JoAnna Brandon . 18463-0-11
☐ 134 UNDER THE SIGN OF SCORPIO, Pat West . . 19158-0-27
☐ 135 SURRENDER TO A STRANGER, Dallas Hamlin 18421-5-12
☐ 136 TENDER BETRAYER, Terri Herrington 18557-2-18

ECSTASY ROMANCES $2.25 each

☐ 450 SWEET REVENGE, Tate McKenna 18431-2-10
☐ 451 FLIGHT OF FANCY, Jane Atkin 12649-5-11
☐ 452 THE MAVERICK AND THE LADY,
  Heather Graham 15207-0-34
☐ 453 NO GREATER LOVE, Jan Stuart 16377-3-28
☐ 454 THE PERFECT MATCH, Anna Hudson 16947-X-37
☐ 455 STOLEN PASSION, Alexis Hill Jordan 18394-4-23

☐ 1 *THE TAWNY GOLD MAN*, Amii Lorin 18978-0-35
☐ 2 *GENTLE PIRATE*, Jayne Castle 12981-8-33

 At your local bookstore or use this handy coupon for ordering:

DELL READERS SERVICE—DEPT. B1144A
P.O. BOX 1000, PINE BROOK, N.J. 07058

Please send me the above title(s). I am enclosing $_____ (please add 75c per copy to cover postage and handling) Send check or money order no cash or COD's Please allow 3-4 weeks for shipment. CANADIAN ORDERS please submit in U.S. dollars

Ms Mrs Mr_____

Address_____

City State_____ Zip_____